THE MORTICIAN'S
ROAD TRIP

THE MORTICIAN'S ROAD TRIP

James D. Loy

The New
Atlantian Library

THE NEW ATLANTIAN LIBRARY
is an imprint of
ABSOLUTELY AMAZING eBOOKS

Published by Whiz Bang LLC, 926 Truman Avenue, Key West, Florida 33040, USA.

For information contact:
Publisher@AbsolutelyAmazingEbooks.com

ISBN-13: 978-0692518748 (New Atlantian Library, The)
ISBN-10: 0692518746

CHAPTER ONE

azlo Y. Wetzo was blitzed – absolutely hammered. He was so blitzed, in fact, that he was having a late afternoon staring match with the man he had just embalmed. The corpse on the receiving end of Lazlo's fixed gaze belonged to J. Duffy Smith, lately of 16 Pussy Willow Road, Moose Wallow, Maine, who had died at the age of ninety-five while shoveling snow. The body had been brought to the town's only funeral home, Styx's Riverside Mortuary, following verification by the county medical examiner that Duffy was, in fact, a goner and that he had died of natural causes. At Styx's, the ambulance squad was told that the owner was out of town, but that the new assistant mortician, one Lazlo Wetzo, was on the job and prepared to sign for Mr. Smith's remains. The body changed hands and the EMTs went for a pizza.

The paperwork that accompanied the body informed Lazlo that Mr. Smith had outlived his wife and all of his family. With no next of kin to consult about burial instructions, Lazlo had checked the mortuary's files and found, to his great relief, that years earlier Duffy had taken out a pre-paid burial plan that specified embalming, then cremation, and then eternity in an urn shaped like a miniature cedar chest. Stretched out on the embalming table, Duffy had just enjoyed (one hopes) the completion of Phase One of that contract. Phase Two, cremation, was scheduled for the next day, when Duffy would slide into a fiery furnace encased in the "best quality" cardboard box that now lay empty under the embalming table. The only deviation so far from the dead man's scripted arrangements was this unauthorized staring match with his mortician – a test of wills that Lazlo had made possible by taping Duffy Smith's eyes open.

An explanation, though certainly not an exculpation, of

Lazlo's unprofessional behavior rests on the fact that, bored and working alone in his boss's absence, he had not only embalmed Mr. Smith that afternoon, but had pretty much done the same to himself by downing a six-pack of freeze-distilled, high alcohol beer over the course of an hour. He really hadn't intended to get juiced, at least not quite as juiced as he was, but each beer had been so tasty and had gone down so smoothly that he'd reached for the next one without thinking. And now, with the full six-pack under his belt, Lazlo found himself so completely waxed that he could no longer be *absolutely* certain that Duffy Smith was really and truly dead. Had the corpse just moved a little, taken a shallow breath, twitched its nose? "Maybe the old codger is still alive and just being stubborn about blinking," thought Lazlo from inside a bulletproof alcohol haze. All the young mortician knew for sure was that he was exhausted and desperately wanted to go to sleep.

"Come on, old guy! Blink so I can take a nap!" sputtered Lazlo, in a voice so high-pitched and slurred that he hardly recognized it as his own. "You know you can't outstare me, even though you're *dead* – or at least I think you're dead. And if you're not dead, say so, dammit!"

Ignoring the taunts, Duffy remained as silent as the tomb he would soon call home and, thanks to the tape on his eyelids (which Lazlo had now completely forgotten about applying), maintained steady eye contact with his tormentor. Rather glassy-eyed contact, but steady.

"Blink, damn you! Blink!" shouted Lazlo, emphasizing each word with a hop that lifted his five-foot-eight-inch, 180-pound body several inches off the floor and brought it crashing back down, rattling the bottles of chemicals stored nearby and making Duffy bounce around on the embalming table. "Blink, blink, blink!" chanted Lazlo, who was getting seriously agitated and also winded from all the hopping. Finally, one last stupendous hop and "BLINK!" caused the corpse to roll right off the table and plop neatly onto its back inside the cremation box. The force of the fall tore the tape off of Duffy's right eyelid and it popped shut. He lay there winking at Lazlo, apparently delighted with the really good joke of being embalmed alive.

"Holy shit!" yelped Lazlo, stumbling backwards from the apparently resurrected Duffy. "You *are* alive! Oh crap, Mr. Smith, I swear I didn't know! I'm so, so sorry! That embalming had to hurt! Oh man, Ron Styx is going to kill me!" By now both blitzed and terrified, Lazlo leaned against the wall of the embalming room trembling and gasping for air. Then just as he thought his heart might jump out of his chest, his muscles gave way into a cataplectic episode and he slid smoothly down the wall and onto the floor alongside J. Duffy Smith. A casual observer would have said that both of the recumbent men seemed to be at peace, but that one was winking.

~ ~ ~

Lazlo Yastrzemski Wetzo, novice mortician and narcoleptic, had arrived in Moose Wallow three months prior to the scene described above. He had come by way of Boston, where he was born; Denver, where he went to college (and in his leisure time, helped with the effort to get pot legalized); and Chicago, where he flunked out of graduate school. (The actual names of the universities he attended have been withheld to protect the innocent and to avoid lawsuits.) Lazlo was the offspring of avid Boston sports fans: hence his middle name, an act of homage to the legendary Red Sox left fielder. His first name reflected the family's Hungarian roots: King Lazlo (or László) ruled Hungary from 1077 to 1095. Our Lazlo's dad, Arnie Wetzo, had originally wanted to name his son Attila – Attila the Hun being another early king from the region that is now Hungary – but the boy's mother would have none of it. A devotee of alliteration and country music, Edith Wetzo's preferred name for her son was Willy Waylon. The parents compromised on Lazlo.

Before he reached legal adulthood, Lazlo was forced to suffer through twelve years of public schooling in Boston and learned, in his humble opinion, absolutely nothing. (His study habits more or less guaranteed that outcome.) Then, because he wasn't keen on going straight into a lifetime of serving burgers, Lazlo talked his parents into underwriting a shot at college. To everyone's great surprise, and despite the fact that it took six years to accomplish, he eventually earned a Bachelor of Science degree in physical anthropology.

Now physical anthropology is a pretty broad field and Lazlo's specialty, insofar as B. S. graduates can be said to *have* specialties, was paleoanthropology, the study of human evolution and its fossil evidence. He dreamed of going to Africa in search of the remains of our pre-human ancestors. "How absolutely, stunningly cool it would be to have a fossil named after you," he mused. "*Australopithecus wetzoi* has such a nice ring to it!" It was a wonderful fantasy, but just as many "a beautiful theory [is] slain by an ugly fact" (T. H. Huxley's, not mine), in the end, Lazlo's dream of fossil-hunting glory was torpedoed by his inability to do PhD-level math. After one disastrous year of post-grad work, Bill Ellison, Dean of the Graduate School, advised him that returning the next fall would be pointless. Lazlo protested, arguing quite correctly that "even Darwin had trouble with math," but his protests fell on deaf ears. And so it came to pass that twenty-six-year-old L. Y. Wetzo found himself entering the terrible job market of 2013 with a smile, a full head of hair, a passable knowledge of human anatomy, and a terminal B. S. degree in physical anthropology.

To put Lazlo's predicament in a bit of perspective, back in the late 1970s there was a TV show called *Welcome Back, Kotter*. In one episode, the central character, Gabe Kotter, asked his wife why she didn't get a job. Her reply went something like this: "But Gabe, I'm an anthropologist. There *are* no jobs for anthropologists!" And that, in a nutshell, was precisely the position in which Lazlo Wetzo found himself after washing out of grad school. You have an undergraduate degree in physical anthropology? Can you say, "Would you like fries with that?" Lazlo had come full circle and found himself facing a lifetime in the fast food industry.

For a while, the stark reality of his situation knocked the wind out of Lazlo. Although usually upbeat and optimistic, now he was down on himself, down on life, down in the dumps. To his parents' dismay, he moved back to Boston and made a bachelor apartment out of their basement. Arnie and Edith put up with their son's presence for a year, but finally, despite the fact that he represented the entire Wetzo clan's last hope of posterity, they invited him to work out his destiny elsewhere.

"For God's sake, Lazlo, get a job, *any* job!" said his exasperated father. "And then move out! You're driving your mother and me nuts, not to mention eating us out of house and home."

"But Dad," whined Lazlo, putting down the book he was reading. "I've got no marketable skills."

"Seven years of college and you're telling me you've got no marketable skills? How is that possible? What are you interested in?"

"Well, I like anatomy," said Lazlo, desperately hoping this conversation would end soon.

"Yeah, I can see that from the poster of Kate Upton you've taped to your wall," said Arnie sarcastically (although, secretly, he liked the poster too). "What else?"

"I dunno," shrugged Lazlo. "It sounds stupid, but I'd like a job where I could wear a white lab coat. The girls in my anthro lab told me I look good in a lab coat. Very professional."

"Well, that's just great, son, lab coats and anatomy. But since you're not a candidate for either medical or dental school that leaves you wearing a lab coat while you leer at Kate Upton, which is not an image I care to dwell on. Hey, are you listening to me or am I talking to myself?" ("To yourself," thought Lazlo, wisely not voicing it.) "Put that book down. What is that you're reading, anyway?" asked Arnie.

"It's nothing, just something to kill the time. It's called *Stiff*, if you must know. It's about cadavers. Since it's not about sports, you probably haven't read it," said Lazlo.

"Well, smart ass, you're right, I haven't read it," said Arnie. "Nonetheless, it sounds creepy, if not positively twisted. But hang on a minute. Maybe, just maybe, it gives us another useful clue about the interests of Lazlo Y. Wetzo. Let's put the pieces together. You're interested in dead people, anatomy, and lab coats, right? Can you think of any jobs that combine all three?"

"Look, dad," said Lazlo, "if you're talking about CSI-type stuff, I don't have the technical training for it. Analyzing wounds, determining the cause of death, calculating how long ago somebody died from the kind of maggots feeding on the corpse, I can't do any of that. Forensic anthropologists need to know *a lot* of science."

"Yeah, but I'm not talking about that sort of thing, son. What about working in a funeral parlor? You know, preserving the corpses that come in, making them look good for open-coffin viewing, and like that – all while wearing a white lab coat. You know enough about human anatomy to do that, right?"

"Well, yeah, I suppose," began Lazlo. "But..."

"No buts, son," said his father as he motioned Lazlo toward the latter's ever-present laptop computer. "Google up 'morticians' and see if anybody anywhere is hiring apprentice embalmers. No arguments. Just do it. Now!"

And as luck would have it, there actually were some online ads for entry-level embalmers. One opening was in the badlands of Pennington County, South Dakota, about a million miles from nowhere (Lazlo passed on that one); a second was in Palm Springs, California (Lazlo called, only to be told that the position had been filled: "We had over one hundred applicants," said the cheery woman on the other end); and a third was in Moose Wallow, Maine. The rest, as they say, is history.

~ ~ ~

Moose Wallow, Maine, turned out to be a tiny town between Fort Kent and Eagle Lake. To describe its location as "extreme northern Maine" is an understatement: a six-mile drive puts you in New Brunswick, Canada. Whereas Fort Kent, sitting alongside the St. John River, boasts a population of 4,097 souls, Moose Wallow tops out at 515. And while Fort Kent is home to a thousand-student-strong regional campus of the University of Maine and therefore has the bars, movie theaters, and coffee shops that inevitably accompany a college campus, the liveliest place in Moose Wallow is the Country Girl Diner on Route 11.

Lazlo Wetzo moved to Moose Wallow in January – a bad

idea since the average daytime high for that month is nineteen degrees Fahrenheit and the average nighttime low is five below zero. At the suggestion of his new boss, Mr. Charon Styx (whose mother had been a Greek mythology major), Lazlo found temporary lodging at the Singing Moose Motel on Main Street. Thanks to a wonky thermostat, his room at the S & M Motel (as smirking locals liked to call it) alternated unpredictably between sweltering heat and toe-numbing cold. When the furnace conked out entirely in the middle of the night, the water pipes in Lazlo's bathroom froze solid. It was not an auspicious start.

CHAPTER TWO

It was a bleary-eyed Lazlo Wetzo who wandered into Styx's Riverside Mortuary for his first day of work. Mr. Styx, who invited Lazlo to call him Ron, had gotten there early to help his new assistant get squared away. Lazlo was given a small office to call his own (a former broom closet) and he was provided with embalmers' work clothes: a couple of white lab coats – "YES!!" Fist pump! – to protect his street clothes from preservatives and bodily ilk, rubber gloves, rubber shoe covers, and two pairs of plastic goggles. Ron had gone to the trouble of getting Lazlo's lab coats personalized to match his own, which proudly read, "Ron Styx, SRM Head Mortician." Unfortunately, the seamstress at Logo Lady Embroidery had let Ron down by leaving off a critical "t" on Lazlo's coats. When those garments were delivered, they were found to read, "Lazlo Wetzo, SRM Ass. Mortician." Despite the nice upper body/lower body division of labor implied by the two labels, Ron was not pleased with the Logo Lady's services and told her so. She gave him the coats at half price.

"Sorry about the lab coats," said Ron. "I'd take them back, but you'll probably never wear them outside of the embalming room anyway and you've gotta admit your label's pretty funny."

"Not a problem," said Lazlo. "Thanks for the gear. I figured I'd have to buy all this stuff myself. Either that or do without."

"You're welcome," said Ron. "You don't want to go home at night smelling like you took a bath in formaldehyde. It's impossible to escape picking up some chemical smell, but a lab coat helps. OK, we might as well get you started. Let's go to the back and get down to business."

Lazlo followed his boss into the embalming room, which had its own double-door rear entrance. Ron opened the doors to show Lazlo the Styx's Mortuary hearse parked at the end of a concrete ramp up which the "newly deceased" arrived on gurneys. Then Ron directed Lazlo's attention to the far side of the room where the earthly remains of the mortuary's latest client, sixty-eight-year-old Earnest Pelletier, lay on a stainless steel table tethered to a state-of-the-art embalming station. The station, which was brand-new and Ron's pride and joy, featured hose connections that allowed removal of a corpse's blood and its simultaneous replacement with embalming fluid. It also had a heavy-duty in-sink waste disposal unit for getting rid of non-blood bodily contents; hot and cold water connections; an electric outlet with a waterproof cover; and an exhaust duct that could be connected to the building's ventilation system. There were also drawers for surgical instruments, a shelf for tissue specimens, and a small light fixture in case extra illumination was needed. Dead though he was, Earnest Pelletier looked proud to be lying atop such a fine piece of equipment.

As he gazed down at the corpse, Lazlo experienced a bit of internal second-guessing along the lines of, "What have I gotten myself into?" His musings were cut short by Ron's instructions to cover Mr. Pelletier's private parts with a surgical drape, close his eyes and mouth, and then try to massage a little of the rigor mortis out of his limbs. Then it was time for Lazlo to demonstrate how well he knew his way around a human body.

"OK, Lazlo, it's anatomy time," said Ron Styx. "See if you can find the right carotid artery and jugular vein up near the collarbone. Cut into the body with a careful little incision that won't show under a dress shirt." Lazlo did as he was told and was thrilled (and relieved) to find the two blood vessels pretty easily. "How do you like me now, Dean Ellison?" he thought to himself.

"Great," said Ron, smiling at the kid's success. "Nice work. Now we'll just insert a feed line into the artery for the preservatives and a matching drain line into the vein for the blood. After that, the embalming machine will slowly pump in a mixture of formaldehyde and methanol, which, in turn, will force the blood out."

Once the perfusion had been completed, Ron and Lazlo opened Earnest Pelletier's abdomen and suctioned out the contents of the hollow organs and the chest cavity. It was not the nicest job in the world, but it went quickly with the two of them working together. Finally, when all the tubes had been removed and all the incisions sutured, they washed the body (including the hair), tidied it up, and applied cream to the face to keep it moisturized. Earnest Pelletier was now ready to be dressed and made up for viewing.

"OK, that went pretty smoothly," said Ron. "Of course, Mr. Pelletier was easy since he was intact. Bodies that have been autopsied are trickier since the organs have been removed for inspection by the Medical Examiner. If the M. E. gives us back the organs, we clean them up, soak them in preservatives for a few hours, put them in a viscera bag, and then tuck them into the coffin at the feet of the deceased. Well, I'm hungry! What do you think about a nice juicy burger at the Country Girl? And don't worry, the images of Mr. Pelletier's insides will fade pretty quickly."

"Uh, well," said Lazlo in an embarrassed voice, "a burger sounds good, but actually I'm a bit short of cash until payday. I brought some cheese and crackers when I came in this morning."

Ron shook his head. "Come on, kid. I'm buying. We've got to celebrate your first embalming job, don't we? Grab your coat and gloves. After lunch, I'll show you how to cosmeticize a corpse. We want the Pelletier family to say, 'He looks so lifelike,' when they come to tomorrow's viewing."

And so, conscious of having done a good morning's work, the two morticians went off to focus on *filling* body cavities rather than emptying them.

~ ~ ~

Lazlo liked the Country Girl Diner from the first time he entered the place. It had a nice ambiance, friendly and comfortable, like his favorite bar back in Boston. He had a feeling that after a few visits it would be a place where "everybody would know his name," to paraphrase the song. But if the Country Girl's ambiance felt familiar, its décor was unlike anything Lazlo had ever seen. A huge moose head was mounted on the wall above the bar, its flattened antlers stretching nearly six feet from tip to tip and its glass eyes seeming to follow the restaurant's patrons around the room. Challenging the moose in size, a gigantic canoe was suspended from the ceiling. Other wall decorations included skis, snowshoes, double bit axes, ice skates, hockey sticks, a signed picture of Bobby Orr, old fashioned steel toothed traps, a stuffed beaver, a stuffed pheasant, a clock with a University of Maine black bear logo, and a black bra labeled "Found under Table Three on 6/27/2004."

Lazlo and Ron seated themselves at a corner table and began to look over the menu. ("Is this the infamous Table Three?" wondered Lazlo. He took a quick look underneath, but found only their feet.) When the waitress came over, they ordered burgers, sodas, and chocolate moose pie for dessert.

"If it was the end of the day, I'd buy you a congratulatory drink, Lazlo," said Ron. "But we've got to finish prepping Mr. Pelletier this afternoon and so we'd better stick with soda."

"That's OK," said Lazlo as he looked around at his fellow diners and found quite a diverse slice of humanity. There were lawyers in suits, Harley riders in jeans and leather jackets, après-ski-dressed tourists in town for the snow sports, and youngsters Lazlo took to be U. Maine students down from Fort Kent. With the exception of a big, bearded guy in the opposite corner, it was pretty much a typical pub crowd busily digging into their BLTs and burgers. The bearded guy, on the other hand, would have stood out in any crowd, anywhere. He looked like an escapee from *Duck Dynasty* with his long hair, bushy beard, full camo costume, and Bean boots. Compared to the *Duck Dynasty* guys though, this dude was seriously huge. He looked like he could eat everything on the Country Girl menu and still be hungry. He was sitting alone and picking his teeth with a Mantis hunting knife.

"Hey, Ron," said Lazlo in a barely audible voice, "who's the Si Robertson type over in the corner? He's straight out of the woods, that's for sure."

"Him? He's the local taxidermist, a really nice guy. I'll introduce you," said Ron, proceeding to wave the hairy guy over.

After giving a return wave and snapping the Mantis into the plastic sheath that he wore on his belt, the bearded man ambled over. As he approached, Lazlo's eyes widened. The newcomer was huge, at least six-feet-eight-inches tall and weighing north of 250 pounds. His hands were massive. Lazlo scrambled to grab another chair from a nearby table.

"Hi, Ron," said the big guy, "how ya'll doing?"

"Good, Uli, good," said Ron. "But I want you to meet someone. Lazlo Y. Wetzo, meet Uliba Helmsman." Lazlo stood and looked up – way up – into the newcomer's face. His eyes looked friendly enough behind all the facial hair, but who could tell for sure? The two men shook hands as Ron continued the introduction. "Lazlo's my new assistant mortician, Uli. We're just about done getting Mr. Pelletier ready for tomorrow's funeral. You coming?"

"Nah, probably not," said Helmsman after shaking hands with Lazlo. "I'm working on a she bear that's due down south in a few weeks. Besides, I barely knew Mr. Pelletier, 'though I hear he was a fine man. So, Lazlo – it is Lazlo, right? – how the hell did you end up in Moose Wallow? You a native Mainer or an immigrant like the rest of us."

"Oh, you know, you go where the work is," shrugged Lazlo. "I studied anthropology in college and learned a lot of anatomy. Now I'm applying it to embalming bodies for Mr. Styx. And you're right about me not being a Mainer. I'm from Boston."

"Hey, a Beaner! That's good. We like Beaners up here, don't we, Ron?" roared Helmsman as he clapped Lazlo on the back, nearly dislodging two front teeth in the process. "So what's the 'Y' stand for, Lazlo? How come you're hiding your middle name behind an initial?"

"Well, it's a little embarrassing," said Lazlo, coloring slightly. "My middle name is Yastrzemski, after Carl, the baseball player. My folks are big Boston sports fans and this was their way of honoring a guy they worshiped. My dad even called me Yaz for a while. Parents can be weird sometimes. How about you? Where does the name 'Uliba' come from?"

At Lazlo's question, Ron started to chuckle and Helmsman looked sheepish. Then the big man laughed and said, "OK, now *I'm* gonna let *you* in on an embarrassing secret, one that's even worse than being named Yastrzemski. The story my mother tells is that when I was born my daddy's first reaction was to go on a bender to celebrate the arrival of his first son. When he finally got around to coming to the hospital to take a look at me, he was still a little bit scrooched and he said the first thing that came into his mind – 'Well, he's an ugly little bastard, if I ever saw one.' Mom didn't much appreciate the remark, but the name stuck. 'Uliba' combines the first letters of 'ugly little bastard.' It looks like we're both the victims of our parents' bad jokes. You should consider yourself lucky to have been named after a Hall of Famer. Anyway, most folks just call me Uli."

"'Uli' it is then," said Lazlo, beginning to warm to this bearded giant who he judged to be in his early thirties. "Why don't you pull up a chair and join us? We're still waiting for our meals."

"Yeah, sure. I'm done eating, but I'll sit for a minute," said Uli with a smile. "But now listen, Lazlo, if you like anatomy, you'll have to come over to my taxidermy shop some time and have a look at all my critters. Bears, foxes, moose, people – they're all pretty much the same under the skin."

"I'd like that," said Lazlo. "We dissected monkeys in college, but I've never cut into anything that's not a primate."

"I can give you a chance to change that," grinned Uli. Just then the food was delivered and conversation gave way to eating.

CHAPTER THREE

On a Saturday morning three days later, Lazlo made the short drive to the outskirts of Moose Wallow and Uli Helmsman's taxidermy shop. Uli had said that he operated out of a small building next to a red farmhouse and those directions, plus the stuffed groundhog atop Uli's mailbox, enabled Lazlo to find the shop on his first pass. As he pulled his white panel van into the dirt parking area, Lazlo noticed a deer – a nice eight-point buck – and a domestic pig, both hanging gutted at the edge of the woods. He made a mental note to ask Uli about the pig. "Why would anyone want to have a pig stuffed?" he wondered. "A wild boar, maybe, but not a white Yorkshire."

Lazlo got out of the van and strolled over to the shop's entrance. Above the door, there was a sign that read Moose Wallow Wildlife and he could hear someone inside singing the Eagles' hit song, *Take It Easy*, accompanying the band's CD. He walked in and gave a shout.

"Hey, Uli!"

A huge, hairy head looked around from behind a partially stuffed bear. The animal had been posed in a very un-lifelike and rather comical stance: sitting up with its forelimbs raised, paws together, and smiling (or as nearly as a bear's muzzle can be sculpted into a smile). Uli grinned when he spotted Lazlo's quizzical stare.

"She's going to be the mascot of a Christian bookstore down in Georgia," he shouted over the music. "I guess they're going to put an open book in her paws. She needs to look cute and friendly so she won't scare the kids. Once she's done, I'll be making a run down south to deliver her."

"Oh," shouted Lazlo in return. "Going to a bookstore, huh? For a bear, you'd expect a more ferocious pose, but I guess that explains it."

"The customer is always right," bellowed Uli.

After turning down the music enough to allow a conversation, Uli advanced and extended his hand. "Hey, man," he said. "Glad you could make it. Come over and take a close look at old Bookworm Bear here. Can I offer you a joint?" He gestured toward a short glass jar that held several marijuana cigarettes.

"Well, heck, I don't mind if I do," said Lazlo, extracting a nice doobie from the jar. "So this is what you do for fun on weekends? Get high and stuff dead things?"

"Yeah, that's pretty much it," grinned Uli. "When there's just the critters and me out here, we usually put on the Eagles or the Grateful Dead and toke out. I know my Southern Baptist mama would be ashamed of me, but I can't see any harm in it. Matter of fact, I'm convinced a little Mary Jane is good for what ails you."

"Wow! This is great weed, man!" enthused Lazlo. "I spent a year or so working to get pot legalized in Colorado and I tried a lot of different varieties in the process. This is about the best stuff I've ever smoked! Is it local?"

"Oh yeah," said Uli with a knowing smile. "These Maine woods grow good weed if it's cultivated properly."

"Outstanding!" said Lazlo, who could already feel a little buzz coming on. "But listen, tell me what's with the pig hanging in your yard? You're not going to stuff that too, are you?"

"Nah, man," said Uli with a laugh (he had started smoking before Lazlo arrived and was well into the "everything is funny" phase of getting stoned). "A guy up in Fort Kent brought the pig in for me to kill, butcher, and package for the freezer. Although my expenses are pretty low out here, the taxidermy business is still too erratic for that to be my only source of income. I also provide abattoir services for the locals. Mostly they bring in deer carcasses, especially during hunting season, but I get a fair number of pigs too. Folks around here love to serve a roast suckler on either Christmas or New Year's."

"Cool, very cool," said Lazlo, lighting up a second fatty. "Listen, Uli, you got anything to drink? My mouth is going seriously dry."

"Sure. There's plenty of beer in the 'fridge. Help yourself," said Uli as he gestured toward a refrigerator against the wall. "I do believe I'll have one too."

As the men smoked their joints and drank their beers, they swapped biographical information, each taking the measure of the other.

"So you're a college guy, huh?" said Uli. "That's great. Me? I've taken a few courses here and there, but never earned a degree or anything like that. Hell, I barely made it out of Avery County High School. See, like you, I moved to Maine from somewhere else. In my case, that somewhere was Little Possum, North Carolina, a tiny little piss-ant town in the mountains. My people are all Tar Heels – Southern Baptist, Republican, conservative Tar Heels, to be exact. Maybe you've heard of my late cousin, the senator?"

"Les E. Helmsman?" said Lazlo, his eyes widening. "You're kidding me! You're not really kin to Senator Les E. Helmsman, are you, Uli?"

"Damn straight, I am," said Uli, "and proud of it. Cousin Les E. knew what he liked and what he didn't. He was a good family man and a regular churchgoer who counted Billy Graham as a close friend. He was hard on commies and liberals, 'those damned progressives,' as he called them. You couldn't get much further to the political right than Cousin Les E.

"But you know," Uli continued, "what I always liked best about Cousin Les E. was his opposition to 'Big Government' and his strong stand for states' rights and individuals' rights. He was convinced that the federal government poses a threat to individual Americans and I think he was onto something. When the FEMA agents come swooping down in their black helicopters and drag us all off to those prison camps they've got scattered all over the country disguised as railroad yards, folks'll finally say, 'Well, damn! Old Les E. Helmsman was right after all.' Of course, it'll be too late then."

"Well," said Lazlo, "you lost me completely with that black-helicopters-and-FEMA stuff. Someday when I'm not stoned, I'll ask you to explain that. For now, I guess we'll just have to agree to disagree on politics. You're gonna hate this, but I'm one of those liberal Bostonians whose kinfolks have voted Democratic ever since Christ was a corporal. But why'd you leave North Carolina and move to Maine? I've always heard the Appalachians are beautiful."

"Western North Carolina is God's country, that's for sure," said Uli. "Nice people, the most beautiful scenery anywhere, and good food. By the way, have you tried the grits at the Country Girl yet? If not, don't bother! They'd gag a maggot. Anyway, the main problem back in North Carolina a few years ago was that jobs, especially good ones, were almost impossible to find. After high school, I worked construction for a couple of years – big guys like me are always in demand for construction jobs that involve a lot of heavy lifting – but that got old and so I took a job as a general flunky shoveling elephant shit at the Southlands Zoo near Charlotte. I made some good friends at the zoo, but it wasn't too long before the itch to change careers came over me again. By then, I'd met a guy in Charlotte who did taxidermy for a living and it looked like fun. So I found me a taxidermy school in Banner Elk, not far from my hometown, got trained in the art of making everything look like a stuffed frog, and set up shop for myself."

"But how the hell did you get from North Carolina to Maine?" asked Lazlo as he took a deep drag on his joint. "Why aren't you still down south where they serve good grits?"

"Now don't make fun of grits, little fella," said Uli with a wink. "Shrimp and grits? Man, we're talking manna from Heaven. But, jokes aside, the answer to your question is pretty simple. I followed a cute little girl up here only to have her dump me for a CPA. I took that pretty hard and stayed stoned a long time, but when I sobered up I found, much to my surprise, that I liked Moose Wallow just fine. There aren't a lot of people up here and in that way it's like Avery County. And the folks around here mind their own business. If I want to smoke dope and roll in the snow in my birthday suit, that's OK with them – so long as I don't do it on Main Street."

"And you make ends meet through a combination of stuffing animals and butchering them," said Lazlo, whose eyes were now distinctly glazed and who had a fierce case of the munchies.

"Yep. The abattoir bit was an add-on, like I said. Which brings up a question for you, Mr. Anthropologist. How come most modern people – even folks who like their steaks nice and rare – are squeamish about slaughtering their own meat? I thought being the descendants of killer apes was a deep part of human nature. Hell, Stanley Kubrick sure made it look like that in *2001*."

"Whoa! Killer apes? You just morphed into Robert Ardrey, man! And I thought you claimed not to be well educated," said Lazlo.

"Well, I read a fair bit," said Uli, "and I know Ardrey's work and most of the rebuttals that claim humans are peaceful creatures deep down. So what do you think? Have we evolved to 'make love, not war' like bonobos, or the opposite, like chimps?"

Lazlo opened his mouth to answer the question, but then, fueled by the marijuana, he suddenly found Uli's interrogation about human evolution remarkably funny. He could remember similar drunken conversations with his grad school cronies and they usually got sidetracked into the complexities of bonobo sex – and some of that *was* remarkably funny. In any event, Lazlo now threw his head back and brayed with laughter until the tears streamed down his face. Then, with only a slurred, "Uh oh," as a warning that something was about to happen, he slid out of his chair and onto the shop's floor. He lay there twitching.

Uli had joined in Lazlo's laughter even though he didn't know quite what the joke was and now he continued to chuckle as he waited for his new friend to climb back into his chair. When that didn't happen, he prodded Lazlo with the toe of his boot.

"Hey, Lazlo, what's up man? You taking a nap or something? Get up, bro. That floor's got to be cold."

When Lazlo made no move to get up, Uli checked his pulse and then held a mirror up to his mouth to see if he was breathing. When both tests confirmed that the young embalmer was still among the living, Uli covered him with a blanket and ambled off to get another joint.

~ ~ ~

Twenty minutes later, Lazlo finally regained control of his muscles and sat up. Fully conscious during the cataplectic episode, he had been aware of Uli hauling him up off the floor and onto an old sofa. The taxidermist now sat staring at him from a nearby chair.

"What the hell just happened, Laz?" asked Uli. "One second you're sitting there laughing your ass off, the next second you've keeled over, and now you've come back to life and don't look much the worse for wear. What gives?"

"Sorry, Uli. Sometimes I can see these episodes coming on, but that one snuck up on me. The fact is that about a year ago I was diagnosed as having narcolepsy. It's a medical condition related to the fact that I don't sleep well at night. Not getting enough nighttime sleep means I'm drowsy during the day and liable to nod off at any time. And then there's the passing out stuff. Sometimes when something startles me or cracks me up or pisses me off – the doctors say any strong emotion can do it – I go limp for a while. It's called a cataplectic episode. Mine tend to pass off quickly and I come right back to normal. And get this, I'm completely conscious throughout the whole thing. So far, I haven't hurt myself flopping over."

"Wow, man. Narcoleprosy, huh? That's a new one on me," said Uli, shaking his head in wonder. "And somehow cats are involved when you pass out?"

"Nacro*lepsy*, Uli, not narco*leprosy*," corrected Lazlo. "I don't wake up with skin lesions, thank God. And the collapses are called *cataplexy*. They've got nothing to do with actual pussycats."

"Jeez, Laz, if you're always sleepy, how can you drive? A fit of road rage could make you topple over, right?" said Uli, concerned for his new friend.

"Well, yeah," grinned Lazlo, "there's something to that. I try to be extra careful about driving and I avoid it if I'm really tired. So far, I haven't had any meltdowns behind the wheel."

"That's good," said Uli. "But what about smoking weed? Does that make you more likely to go cata-something?"

"Cataplectic," corrected Lazlo, "and I suppose the answer is 'yes,' if only because everything gets so funny when you're stoned and the silly giggles can bring on a collapse. But if you think I'm giving up ganja just because I occasionally topple over, you're wrong. Before I do that, I'll start wearing padded clothing to cushion the falls. And speaking of weed, I think I'm a joint behind you, so I'd better get another."

The two men continued smoking and talking until mid-afternoon, when it dawned on them that they were ravenous. A late lunch at the Country Girl soon took care of that.

CHAPTER FOUR

Baz Rathbone (or Percy Sanders, according to his birth certificate) sat behind his desk at PWADS, Inc. in Rankin, New York. The acronym stood for Penny-Wise After Death Services and for simplicity's sake it was pronounced "wads," the "P" being silent as in "pseudo" (which describes precisely the sort of business it was – or wasn't, depending on one's point of view). Although the cheap marquee sign above the office door indicated that PWADS was incorporated, that claim was misleading. In Baz Rathbone's opinion, incorporation would have been an unnecessary expense and, more importantly, it might have attracted unwanted official attention.

Baz was a small, wiry man in his mid-fifties who looked exactly like the con man he was. At work, he wore a cheap suit, cheap tie, and cheap shoes – indeed, everything about B. Rathbone, Mortician, was cheap. He was rapidly losing his hair and should have bought a nice toupee, but – you guessed it – he was too cheap, and instead tried unsuccessfully to cover his bald spot with a comb-over. Completing the image of a shifty character, Baz's right eye had a tendency to wander, which made it difficult to "look him in the eye" during a conversation.

Baz's secondary interest in life – his first was making money – was riding his Harley-Davidson Sportster around the upstate New York countryside. On weekends, he would dress up in boots, jeans, and a leather jacket with "Born to Cremate" stenciled on it, and hit the road early. At biker gatherings, he went by the name of "Coffin."

Sitting opposite Baz on this particular morning was Mrs. Edna Blyth, whom he was helping to fill out the contract to have her late husband cremated. Edna was vacillating between buying a plain wooden box for her Mortimer's cremains or a ceramic urn shaped like a lighthouse. Baz was doing his best to talk her into the more expensive container.

"Think how nice the lighthouse urn will look on your mantle, Mrs. Blyth," said Baz in his oily-tongued professional voice. "Every time you look at it, you'll think of your late husband sending down a guiding light from Heaven."

"I'm not all that sure my husband is in Heaven, Mr. Rathbone," said Edna, who had given up trying to figure out which of the mortician's eyes to look at and was staring firmly at the desk. "Besides that, he never was much good at directions. If I have to count on him as my navigator to Heaven, I'll probably get lost. I loved him, but Morty Blyth had no use for church. Besides that, he drank too much, swore too much, and worked as little as possible. I'll remember him mostly for being a couch potato. You don't have an urn shaped like a La-Z-Boy recliner, do you?"

"Well now, Mrs. Blyth," said Baz in that same unctuous voice, "I'm sorry to say that I don't carry such an urn as a standard item. Of course, I could have one specially made for you, but it would cost extra."

"No," said Edna. "Let's just settle on the wooden box. If I had wanted to spend a lot of money on Morty, I wouldn't be here talking to you, now would I?"

"OK, a wooden box it is. Now what size would you like? Are you going to keep all of your husband's cremains or do you plan to scatter some?" asked Baz, barely concealing his disappointment over her choice of containers.

"Lord, no, I'm not keeping all of him. I'll be dumping most of Morty's ashes into the Hudson the first time nobody's looking. I just need a little keepsake box."

"Fine. One small handcrafted wooden box for $39.99. Just note on the form, 'wooden box, small,'" sighed Baz, who hated to see a prize fish like Edna nibble at the bait and then swim away.

Once the decision about the urn had been made, the rest of the details concerning Mortimer Blyth's cremation were quickly completed. His widow specified that there would be no funeral service or committal of the ashes. "Just do him up, give me what's left, and we're done," said Edna, who seemed anxious to close out the Mortimer part of her life, as well as the Baz Rathbone part. She signed the contract, and then wrote out a check made payable to PWADS, Inc. and passed it over to Baz, who was also anxious to get on with *his* life.

"Thank you, Mrs. Blyth," said Baz as he ushered her to the door. "Your husband's cremains will be ready for pick-up tomorrow afternoon. I'll mail you a copy of the contract as soon as I can. My secretary is out sick and so the paperwork is stacking up."

After the woman had gone, Baz Rathbone tidied his desk and checked his schedule. Another new widow was due in a half hour, but he had time to pop in next door to the Flintlock Bar for a quick drink. As he glanced around the nicely equipped office – his barely overlapping visual fields allowing almost the entire space to be scanned without moving his head – he was satisfied. "Not too shabby for a con man," thought Baz. Nice furnishings made the place look legitimate to his customers, a firm they could trust to give their loved ones a proper send-off to eternity. Chuckling to himself about looks sometimes being deceiving, Baz locked the door behind him on his way to the bar.

PWADS, Inc. was a storefront business on a down-at-the-heels street in a down-at-the-heels town deep in the Adirondack Mountains. Rankin, New York, had had its economic heyday many years ago and now its inhabitants lived close to the bone, making sure every penny counted. On one side of PWADS there was a secondhand clothing store, while on the other side there was the decidedly questionable Flintlock Bar. The town was the perfect location for a scam artist like Baz Rathbone.

You see, Baz wasn't really in the cremation business, but rather the bone business – or more precisely, the skull business. When a corpse like Morty Blyth's came into his possession because the survivors wanted or needed to save money, Baz would typically bury most of it on his farm up in Owl Hollow, keeping back only the skull. After a few days, he would give the grieving family an urn full of wood ashes, along with his deepest sympathy. Since almost no one ever looked at the contents of a cremation urn, much less had them analyzed to be sure they were human ashes, Baz was now eight years into his little scam without being discovered, although he had taken the precaution of changing counties a couple of times.

Unlike the post-cranial portions of the bodies that passed through his hands, Baz treated the skulls with extreme care. These were carefully emptied, defleshed, degreased, and bleached. The lower jaw was attached to the cranium with small metal rods and springs. Then the skulls were advertised for sale – discreetly, guardedly, and mostly by a word spoken in the right ears – at prices that were a fraction of what one would pay to legitimate skeletal material outlets such as Skulls Unlimited or The Bone Room. Potential buyers included skinheads, punk rock fans, 'real' Goths and 'mall' Goths, street gangs and other fraternal organizations, and practitioners of the occult arts, to name a few. All of these folks and more loved to wear skull jewelry, skull-decorated clothes, and skull tattoos. Skulls were "in." Skulls were cool. They said, "I'm baaad," like no other symbol in American – indeed, global – culture. And if there was anything better than *wearing* a skull, it was *owning* one. Think of it, a genuine human head to display on your coffee table or trophy shelf! "Wicked pissah, bro!" With all this demand, Baz Rathbone had no trouble finding a market for his wares. In a good week, he might sell a couple of skulls at $750 a pop (about half what the legit dealers were asking) and that, along with what he was paid for supposed cremations, gave him an annual income just under six figures. The work was easy and the rewards substantial. Despite those discarded torsos and limbs in the woods, Baz slept well at night.

Of course, one might ask why not put those discarded lower bodies to use as well and earn even more money? After all, full human skeletons were selling for upwards of $5,000 online. Baz had found, however, that he was not very good at articulating complete skeletons. They tended to end up looking like poorly strung marionettes. And besides, processing full skeletons required more space than he had either at the office or at the farm, and shipping them could be risky. Whole skeletons needed large shipping containers –

containers that might attract attention from the Post Office, UPS, or FedEx. Skulls were easy to prepare and small enough to ship without suspicion. And they were light. Shipping costs were minimal. Nope, all things considered, Baz was happy to limit his bone trade to skulls.

Baz's rest at night might not have been so peaceful if he'd known that ending the illegal traffic in human remains had just become a priority for the Boston office of the FBI. Special Agents Steven Nevets and Tom Mot had been assigned to the case and they were beginning to canvas mortuaries all across New England.

CHAPTER FIVE

Special Agents Nevets and Mot had worked as a team for so long they could almost finish each other's sentences. Well, to be absolutely precise, Nevets could do that for Mot, but the latter had trouble returning the favor because Nevets liked to use big words that his partner couldn't understand: real "50-cent" words like *ethics* and *ailurophile*. The difference between the two men was not so much a case of Mot suffering from hippopotomonstrosesquippedaliophobia – the fear of long words – but the result of Nevets being better educated and better read than his counterpart. It was the old story of a state college man versus an Ivy Leaguer.

As Sergeant Joe Friday might have said, "It was noon on Monday, November 6th, when Nevets and Mot were assigned to the case that would ultimately bring them into contact with Lazlo Wetzo." It was cold in Bean Town and a fierce nor'easter was predicted to come sweeping in off the Atlantic before nightfall. Despite the early hour, at the Boston office of the FBI people were starting to pack up and head home. No one wanted to get stranded when Storrow Drive flooded and that included at least one member of the "Palindrome Squad" – the nickname Mot and Nevets had been given because the spelling of each man's name was the same both forwards and backwards: Steven Nevets, Tom Mot.

The case before them was unusual; indeed, neither agent had ever run across anything quite like it in their moderately lengthy careers. It involved the reappearance of a skull supposedly destroyed by cremation years ago. The facts were these. One night in late October, Alice Brady, age thirty-seven and currently living in Boston although formerly a resident of upstate New York, had gone to the Foxy Patriot Lounge down near Boston Harbor. She arrived at the bar with her girl friends, but she left with a skinhead who she knew simply as "Charlie M." Alice accompanied Charlie M. to an economy motel in Quincy and the two of them spent the night there. In the morning, Alice noticed a human skull sitting on the dresser with a half-burned candle on top and a cigar clamped in its teeth. When she took a close look at it, she recognized it as belonging to her late husband, Herman Brady. She was quite sure the skull was Herman's because it had a distinctive bone flap in the back. It seems that ten years earlier Herman had needed a craniotomy to remove a tumor and he had managed to talk the surgeon into making the bone flap the shape of the state of Texas. When Alice accused Charlie M. of possessing her late husband's skull (Herman's tumor had returned and killed him), the skinhead screamed at her, threatened to punch her lights out, and threw her out of the room. Alice called a cab and went home glad to be alive, but three days later she went to the Boston police and reported seeing part of a body that she believed had been cremated. When representatives of the Boston Police Department went with her to the motel, Charlie M. was gone and the management had no information about his identity or whereabouts. The case looked to the BPD like a probable combination of fraud and corpse abuse, and they would gladly have investigated it had it not been for the fact that illegal interstate trafficking of a human body part (Herman's head) also appeared to be part of the crime. Herman had supposedly been cremated in New York State – which specifically prohibits importing and exporting human remains – only to have his head turn up in Massachusetts. All things considered, the BPD preferred to hand the case over to the FBI. Enter agents Nevets and Mot.

"Well, Tom, what do you think?" asked Nevets as he dropped the case file onto his partner's desk.

"I think we ought to head for home like everyone else." (*Weef!*) "Don't you?" replied Mot. "It's getting ready to rain like hell." (*Weef!*)

"Forget the weather," said Nevets. "I was referring to the case of Herman Brady's skull. Besides, I think the forecast is an exaggeration. Storrow Drive is going to drain just fine. Stop worrying about it."

"Yeah, well, I'm not so sure," replied Mot as he gave his nose a couple of twitches. "Ever since the accident, my nose has been a pretty good predictor of the weather, and it's been aching like hell all afternoon." (*Weef!*) "We're gonna get soaked, if you ask me."

The accident to which agent Mot was referring involved the time a few years earlier when he had had the misfortune of being bitten on the nose by a red-bellied piranha fish. Exactly how that had come to pass would require an explanation too lengthy to include here, but the important thing is that Mot had tried to get rid of the fish by shooting it with his service revolver. Unfortunately, his aim had been bad due to the fact that he was hopping around and shaking his head trying to detach his piscine attacker. As a result of trying to jump, shake, and shoot at the same time, he had not only blown the fish away, but part of his nose as well. Plastic surgeons had repaired the nose to the best of their abilities, but it was still a pretty sorry specimen of a human proboscis. Besides being ugly, Mot's reconstructed nose was prone to colds and other infections, and it whistled when he inhaled: *Weef!*. Tom Mot's new nose did one thing well, however, and that was predict the weather. This afternoon it said, "Heavy rain coming."

"Come on, Tom," said Nevets, who was getting a bit exasperated with his junior partner. "We've got time this afternoon to hash out this new case and draw up a plan of attack. I can't justify quitting early just because it's going to rain."

"OK, OK," said Mot in a grumpy voice. "But for the record, it takes me longer to get home to Waltham than it does for you to get to your apartment in Back Bay." (*Weef!*) "Anyway, give me the file. What's your take on it?" (*Weef!*)

"To me," said Nevets, "it looks first of all like a clear case of fraud. Somebody took Mrs. Brady's money and then failed to fulfill a verbal agreement to cremate *all* of her late husband's body. Too damn bad she doesn't have a copy of a written contract for cremation services since such a document might tell us a lot. But she doesn't, so that's that. Anyway, the fraud was apparently followed by criminal abuse of her husband's corpse. I'm guessing the head was removed from the body, defleshed, and emptied of its brains. Then the skull was cleaned and dried prior to being sold on the black market."

"Jeez Louise, Steve," said Mot with a grimace and an indignant *Weef!* "Who the hell would do that and who the hell would *buy* a black market human skull?"

"Skinheads, occultists, some bikers, Indiana Jones fans," answered Nevets. "Not to mention starving artists in need of an anatomical model, weird scientists looking to add to their bone collections, and, of course, Tampa Bay fans."

"Whoa!" said Mot, holding up his hands and *Weef!*ing loudly. "If there are so many different kinds of skull freaks out there, how do we get started checking them out?"

"My suggestion is that we start from the supply end and focus on possible buyers later," said Nevets. "Mrs. Brady turned over her husband's body and her money to a supposed mortician working out of a storefront in far upstate New York, right?" (Mot nodded his head in agreement. The look on his face said, "How stupid can some people be?") "So," continued Nevets, "I'd say our best bet is to start by interviewing all of the morticians north of Albany. It's going to take a while, that's for sure. I wonder how many there are?"

Mot stopped staring out his window at the rain – which was starting to fall steadily, just as his nose had warned might happen – and flipped open his laptop computer. He proceeded to search Google for a list of upstate New York morticians and found that there were dozens and dozens of them. Mot sighed and *Weef!*ed loudly.

"Shit, Steve. This is going to take forever," he muttered. "But I guess there's nothing to do but get started. What do you think, road trip?"

"Yeah, I'd say so," agreed Nevets. "Why don't you swing by my place around nine tomorrow morning? I drove the last time, remember?"

"Nine o'clock, it is," said Mot. "Now let's get out of here before Storrow Drive turns into a watery grave."

CHAPTER SIX

It was Sunday afternoon and Norman McLaughlin was doing his usual weekend cleaning in Bone Room 2. Carefully reaching up to one of the display shelves, he lifted a *Papio cynocephalus* skull off its stand and gave it a thorough dusting. The monkey's long canines were still nicely pointed and Norm was careful not to chip the fragile enamel. Having finished cleaning the baboon skull, he carefully tucked it back into its space between the head of a capybara ("That one cost a lot of money," he thought to himself) and that of an armadillo. It took several hours each week to dust his entire bone collection, but it was worth the effort. His prized specimens fairly gleamed as he looked around the room.

And it was a magnificent collection by any measure. Norman had been "into bones" and other biological items since he was a kid and his specimens now numbered in the thousands. They had stood him in good stead as reference material during his undergrad studies in biology and later during his graduate nursing courses. But far beyond simply being items for study, they were treasured items to be looked at, touched, smelled, and yes, sometimes even tasted. (For some reason, bear bones are saltier than deer bones.) His collection gave Norman an enormous feeling of accomplishment. It gave purpose to his bachelor's existence, something his career had thus far failed to do.

Norm McLaughlin was a fifty-something surgical nurse and a relatively new resident of Maine. He worked at a clinic just north of Bangor and lived in a spacious old farmhouse just ten minutes away. Maine being Maine, in just that short drive Norm went from an urban setting to deep woods. His two-story house sat atop a low hill and was Victorian in its design, featuring a rectangular tower rising above the front porch (i.e., it looked sufficiently like the Bates Motel that you didn't want to pop in for a quick shower). Norm shared the

33

house with a shaggy Maine coon cat named Red Skelton and a Nubian goat named Bill Grogan.

Milquetoast would probably have been the first adjective to come to mind if any of Norm's co-workers had been asked to describe him. He was short and on the dumpy side, and markedly shy. He tended to wear surgical scrubs both at work and around the house. He had few real friends – "an unprepossessing loner" just about summed him up – but was sufficiently competent in the operating room that the local surgeons were happy to keep him around. Perhaps Norm's most interesting physical feature was the tattoo inside his left wrist that read, "Righty tighty, lefty loosey." (Plumbing had always been his least favorite homeowner's chore.)

Like all of us, Norman had his heroes, the main one being Dr. Robert Broom, an early 20th century physician and paleontologist who was born in Scotland, but who made his name in the South African fossil fields. Norm's admiration for Broom had little to do with the latter's studies of early South African mammals, however, but rather it related to Broom's success at amassing a really magnificent collection of human skulls. True, it was rumored that Broom had sometimes resorted to grave-robbing to obtain new specimens for his collection, but Norm brushed that aside as a minor technicality and/or petty gossip about a great man. Like Broom, Norm McLaughlin thought that when it came to getting a new skull, the end justified the means, assuming the means weren't *way* outside the law. (One other interesting fact about Robert Broom is that besides skulls, he also collected human tissues, especially samples of Jacobson's organ, a tiny accessory bit of tissue in the nose. It was rumored that he occasionally harvested bits of Jacobson's organ from anesthetized and unsuspecting patients. For the record, Norman McLaughlin collected only bones.)

But if Norm was prepared to let Robert Broom off the ethical hook of being a grave robber, he wasn't prepared to go quite that far himself to expand his skull collection. Instead, Norm went online and skulked around the edges of the occult and skinhead worlds, as well as keeping an eye on eBay for likely looking specimens. He also contributed the occasional post to a couple of skull collectors' blog sites, and it was after his last blog post that Norm received the following mysterious email.

> FROM: Director, bestheadsforsale.com
> TO: McHead-Case@gmail.com
> SUBJECT: crania mania
> Dear McHead-Case:
> I may be able to help you add to the collection you recently described online. Send me your phone # by return email and I'll be in touch. FYI, this email address will self-destruct in 24 hours. If you are going to respond to this message, do so promptly.
> Sincerely,
> SGM

Intrigued by the email – and who wouldn't have been? – Norman responded promptly. That evening he received a phone call from a guy who called himself Samuel George Morton. Although Norm's razor-sharp mind figured out at once that it wasn't the real Samuel George Morton, a famous American skull collector who died in 1851, he decided not to question the caller's ID – at least not until he knew more. Their conversation went like this.

(SGM) "Hello, Mr. McHead-Case. I understand that you would like to buy a human skull. Is that correct?"

(NMc) "Yes. Yes, I would. That is, if it's in good shape and not outrageously expensive. I'm not a rich man."

(SGM) "OK, I'm sure we can make this work for you. I'm always ready to negotiate about prices. How does $1000 for a perfect adult male skull strike you? It's got a full set of teeth and if you'd like, I can file down the fangs so they're pointed. I guarantee to make that alteration look one hundred percent natural."

(NMc) "Wow! That sounds great, but the teeth don't need to be filed. I'm too old to be into vampires. But, listen, I'm afraid a thousand bucks is little too rich for my blood. Can you sweeten that price a bit?"

(SGM) "I can let the head go for $750, but without the display stand. Is that better?"

(NMc) "Oh yeah. Now I think we could be talking business. Can you tell me the provenience of the skull? I'd love to get one from Polynesia."

(SGM) "Well, you're out of luck there. It's Caucasian and possibly Scandinavian, but it has an interesting dent over the left eye – a wound from a battle-ax or mace, maybe. Anyway, that's about all I can tell you over the phone. Full details on the specimen's history will, of course, come with the skull. So, do we have a deal or not?"

(NMc) "Oh man, yeah, we have a deal. Seven hundred and fifty for a Viking warrior? I'm definitely having this one. How do we go about completing the transaction?"

(SGM) "Tell you what, how about if I give you a PO box number, you send me a prepaid Visa card for $750, and then I put the skull in the mail the instant the card arrives? Will that work for you?"

(NMc) "Well, I suppose, but how do I know I can trust you? You could cash in the card and then stiff me for the skull."

(SGM) "Please, Mr. McHead-Case, you're insulting me. I've been in the bone business for several years and have never had a dissatisfied customer. If you don't want the skull, I'm sure someone else will snap it up in a day or two at most."

(NMc) "No, hey, wait! I was just trying to be careful, but I sure don't want to let this baby slip through my fingers. Give me your address and I'll go buy the card this very minute. Oh, and one other thing while I've got you on the phone. Do you ever have any ape skulls in stock? I'm very anxious to add either a chimp or orangutan skull to my collection, but I never see them on the market."

(SGM) "I don't have any on hand at the moment, but I'll be happy to check with my zoological suppliers. You do realize that such an item could be pricey, right?"

(NMc) "Yeah, I know that, but I'd gladly spend a whole year's bone budget for an ape head. Please check with your people and let me know if you find one."

(SGM) "Will do, Mr. McHead-Case. OK, for today's purchase, the address is SGM, PO Box 1859, Albany, New York, 32123. I'll be watching the mail for that Visa card. Good day to you."

And that was all there was to it. Baz Rathbone had learned early on that most collectors would rather risk losing their money than let what sounded like a unique specimen slip through their fingers. He had, of course, told a couple of innocent lies during his conversation with Norman. First of all, Baz never included display stands with the skulls he sold, much less *expensive* display stands. And second, the dent above the left eye of the skull under discussion was the result of Baz's cat knocking the head off the mantle and onto the edge of a stone hearth. To Baz, both fibs were justifiable tweaks to his sales pitch.

After hanging up the phone, Norm hopped into his car, drove straight to a Rite Aid drugstore in Bangor, and purchased a prepaid Visa card worth $750. Then he went home and spent an hour rearranging his specimens to make a space for the new skull. When Norman McLaughlin, aka McHead-Case, went to sleep that night, it was with visions of Viking warriors dancing in his head.

~ ~ ~

Ten days later, the mailman delivered a small and very light package. Inside was perhaps the most beautiful human skull Norman had ever seen. The gouge above the left eye was deep and sharp edged; in Norm's opinion, it was precisely the sort of injury a mace or war club would have caused. He was delighted with his new acquisition and wasted no time installing it in the place of honor among his other specimens. And there was one other item in the box: a note that read, "Searching for an ape skull. Will be in touch. SGM"

CHAPTER SEVEN

It was March 31st in Moose Wallow, Maine, and unreasonably cold – or so it seemed to the town's assistant mortician. Mud season was just around the corner, but winter was being tenacious. It was the kind of weather when you wanted to be sure you took on enough alcohol to keep your blood from freezing. At least that was Lazlo Wetzo's opinion and on this particular Saturday night, he and Uliba Helmsman were taking on goodly amounts of anti-freeze at the Country Girl Diner. Each man was on his third beer and just getting started for the evening. Their conversation swung back and forth between making plans for a road trip down south and making estimates of the odds that they could successfully pick up the two young women over at table five. Little did they know that the women, having twigged onto the fact that they were being ogled, were about to do some making of their own, i.e., tracks, out the door.

Lazlo and Uli gave a collective sigh as they watched the women, who were probably coeds up at Fort Kent, head out into the night. There were times when sex sounded better than getting stoned, but then again, getting stoned was so much easier. For one thing, you didn't have to take a giggle weed out to dinner. For another, honey blunts never gave birth to little honey blunts nine months later. Still, maybe bonobos had the right idea, after all.

Uli broke the mood by humming a bar of Willy Nelson's classic, *On the Road Again*. "So, I'd say we go straight down I-95, don't you think?" he asked, as he wiped a bit of beer froth from his beard.

"Huh?" said Lazlo, coming back to earth from a daydream in which he was chasing the two women around his embalming room, all three of them wearing nothing under their white lab coats. "What did you say, bro? Something about being ninety-five?"

"Nah, man," said Uli. "Focus, will you? I'm talking about this here road trip we're gonna take. I'm thinking that we've got three errands to run down south and I-95 is the best way to get there and do them. Now, first of all, Ron Styx wants you to go down to South Carolina and pick up the embalmed body of Mrs. Josie May Sagler, right? Mrs. Sagler's grieving family is wintering over in Hilton Head, but they want to grant her final request to be buried in Fort Kent. Well, the straightest shot from here to Hilton Head is US 1 to Houlton, where we can pick up I-95, and then it's pedal-to-the-metal right on down to South Carolina. If you get to Savannah, you've overshot Hilton Head. Anyway, after loading Mrs. Sagler, we cut cross-country over to Augusta, Georgia, where we deliver the Bookworm Bear to the All Creatures Great and Small bookstore. All Creatures is a Christian bookstore and its owners figure Bookworm Bear is going to be a big hit. They tell me that their customers enjoy shootin' God's critters and reelin' in God's fish second only to reading the Bible."

"My Uncle Artie, who lives out on Martha's Vineyard, has taken to reading the Bible a lot lately," said Lazlo absentmindedly. "He has a preacher friend who claims God's real name is Yolanda and that Yolanda zaps bad people with earthquakes. I think Uncle Artie is feeling sinful in his old age and trying to avoid getting zapped. It's all pretty weird, if you ask me."

"'Kum ba yah, Yolanda,' huh?" said Uli. "I'll have to give that one some thought, but it does roll nicely off the tongue. Anyway, to get back to the main topic – namely, our road trip – from Augusta we shoot straight up to Charlotte and pick up Clyde, the dead orangutan that the Southlands Zoo wants me to stuff. It seems old Clyde was a great favorite at the zoo and they want to display his preserved remains in the monkey house. And from Charlotte, we just complete the loop by taking I-85 to I-95 and then home. A piece of cake, don't you think?"

"Why not do it the other way around and get Clyde first?" asked Lazlo. "Then we could deliver the bear, get Mrs. Sagler, and spend a day or two in Charleston on the way home. They've got some seriously good restaurants down there – not to disparage the good old Country Girl, mind you."

"That might work," said Uli, "but it would mean your van would be parked in Charleston for a couple of days with a dead person and a dead ape in the back. And if the coast happens to get a nice spring heat wave, then your little panel truck could take on a real 'air,' if you get my drift. Remember that I don't know what condition old Clyde is going to be in and if he's whiffy, any delay could make for a long run home up the East Coast."

"Yeah, yeah, I see your point," said Lazlo. "OK, we'll do it your way. Go get us another round of brewskis and let's talk timing."

"I'm on it," said Uli as he headed to the bar, whence he emerged two minutes later with a refreshed pitcher.

"I'd say let's hit the road in a couple of weeks," said Lazlo. "Mrs. Sagler is 'on ice' so to speak and can be picked up at our convenience. Plans for her funeral at this end have yet to be made. I'm assuming Clyde is equally 'on ice' in the zoo's morgue. Which only leaves Bookworm Bear. When will she be ready to go?"

"I've hit a couple of glitches with old Bookworm," said Uli, "so the job is going to take at least another month. Without doubt, however, she'll be ready to roll by May 1st. She's going to look good when she's finished, if I do say so myself."

"Excellent," said Lazlo with a grin. "I'm sure she's a prize winner. Anyway, May 1st, it is. I'll let Mr. Styx know on Monday so he can alert the South Carolina Saglers. And when we get a little closer, I'll get the van serviced so we don't break down on the interstate."

They drank their beers in silence for a few minutes, each man occupied with his own thoughts. Then Lazlo said, "So tell me, Uli, what's your take on religion? Do you take after your illustrious cousin and identify yourself as a Southern Baptist? Or like a good friend of mine down in Rhode Island, do you attend Bedside Baptist every Sunday morning?"

"Well, I'll tell you," said Uli after a thoughtful pause, "I'd say I'm more a 'hoper' than a real believer. I *hope* God exists and if he – or she – does exist, then I *hope* I'm not screwing up my life so badly that I end up spending eternity being toasted like a marshmallow. I just try my best to live a do-unto-others/turn-the-other-cheek/leave-only-your-footprints kind of life and hope that's enough. Deep down, I'm pulling for the Hindus to be right about everybody being reincarnated over and over. I'd like to come back as a bear and meet old Bookworm's kin so I could make sure they're not carrying any grudges about me stuffing her. What about you, Yolanda and all your Uncle Artie's weird stuff beside the point."

"I guess I'm in about the same boat as you," said Lazlo. "I was raised to be a good Catholic back in Boston, but I got to the point where the Church had too many rules and 'litmus tests' for my liking. Then I went off to college and majored in anthropology and learned about cultural relativity, which, with regard to religion, pretty much says that all cultures' faiths are about equally valid – so long as they work in their individual contexts. Religion is a funny thing to think about, particularly when you're high. On a field trip to Mexico a few years ago, I chewed a couple of magic mushrooms and for a while I thought I *was* God. But then, like Carlos Castenada, I turned into a raven and flew off. Jeez, what a headache I had the next day!"

"Magic mushrooms, eh?" said Uli with a laugh. "I've always wondered if they grew magic mushrooms on Patmos back in St. John's day. That could explain a lot about his vision, if you get my drift."

Lazlo gave a whoop of laughter. "Well, if you're going to blaspheme like that you're liable to get us both killed by a bolt of Yolanda's lightning. But I don't want to die thirsty, so push that pitcher over this way."

CHAPTER EIGHT

Agents Nevets and Mot were getting very, very tired of interviewing upstate New York morticians. After giving it some thought, they had decided to begin their search for the suspected skull trafficker(s) *in* Albany, rather than north of the state capitol. Since there turned out to be a couple of dozen morticians operating in the Albany-Troy-Schenectady triangle, their investigation quickly turned into strenuous uphill work. Nobody wanted to talk, everyone was rushed, dead bodies needed urgent attention, and grieving families could not be put off. It was like prying information out of the dead, so to speak. Tom Mot, who often daydreamed of quitting the FBI for a less demanding career, struck "mortician" off his list.

Each Monday morning, Nevets and Mot would rendezvous at the Boston FBI office and then car pool for the three-hour drive to New York State. They would live out of their suitcases and eat their meals in restaurants or drive-throughs until mid-afternoon on Friday, when they would make the reverse trip back to Boston. In the process of their New York investigation, Nevets and Mot were spending much more time together than ever before, which meant they were getting to know each other *really well*. It was getting old and their nerves were getting frayed. Occasionally, they were even short with each other, as this example shows.

"You snore like a buzz saw, Steve," (*Weef!*) said Mot over breakfast one morning.

"Is that a fact?" said Nevets, his voice betraying a distinct lack of interest in the subject.

"Yeah." (*Weef!*) "The walls in this crappy motel are paper thin and I can hear every breath. It sounds like you're ripping plywood over in your room. I always thought my wife was the world's worst snorer, but you've got her beat. Thank heavens the Bureau gives us enough per diem money to have separate rooms."

"How in hell you can hear me snoring over your own nose whistles is beyond me, Tom," said Nevets, attacking Mot on a point of great sensitivity. "That damn thing sounds like the fife from a fife-and-drum corps."

"Now that's just not a nice thing to say to your partner, Nevets" (**WEEF!**), said Mot rather brusquely. "You know my nose was injured in the line of duty." (*Weeeff!*) "I didn't ask to be bitten on the nose by a damn piranha fish. I wish to God they'd never been created." (*Weef!*)

"Evolved."

"What?" (*Weef!*)

"According to Professor Uxem, the man who owned that fish, piranhas *evolved* – they weren't created," said Nevets and muttered, "dumb ass," under his breath.

"OK, OK! Have it your way." (*Weef!*) "Piranhas *evolved*, but why God let them evolve into such evil little bastards, I have no idea," said Mot.

"I think evolution is an unpredictable, unguided process, Tom. God doesn't *let* creatures evolve one way or another. Depending on environmental conditions, they just change, sometimes into more advanced creatures, sometimes not." During this little biology lesson, Nevets had unconsciously assumed the chest-out-and-head-back professorial posture that Tom Mot had come to hate.

"Do horses' asses also sometimes evolve unguided into more advanced creatures? If so, maybe there's still a chance for you, Nevets," snapped Mot, emphasizing his insult with a long *Weeeeef!* "For goodness sake, you're not being very Christian toward your hard-working partner."

"I'm Jewish," said Nevets.

And so it went. After interviewing twenty-seven morticians and working their way north from Albany as far as Queensbury, they still didn't seem to be making any progress. All of the businesses they'd visited appeared to be legitimate. Each mortuary had been happy to produce meticulous records of recently embalmed bodies, including information about who signed the corpse over for preparation, whether it was readied for burial or cremation, which staff member(s) had done the work, and the date of final disposition. It seemed to Nevets and Mot that you couldn't have removed the nose hairs from one of those corpses without somebody noticing, much less its head.

In particular, the case that had gotten them into this morass of morticians – Charlie M's possession of Herman Brady's supposedly cremated skull – had yet to come to a head, so to speak. Alice Brady was less than helpful. She claimed to have lost all of the paperwork pertaining to Herman's death in a house fire. Furthermore, she couldn't remember many of the details of the case since she was a recovering meth addict and Herman had passed away at the height of her drug use. Alice couldn't even remember what town they were living in when he died, only that it had had two Mexican restaurants.

A search of the obituaries published in the dozen or so upstate newspapers was equally unproductive. Of course, it might have helped the two agents to know that the Bradys were using aliases at the time of "Herman's" demise in order to stay one jump ahead of the New York State Police. The NYSP's Bureau of Criminal Investigation had a long rap sheet on Earnest and Eliza Didlittle, but there was no reason to connect them with the woman now calling herself Alice Brady and her headless husband. It was all exceedingly frustrating. A few nights after the quarrel described above, during one of their increasingly rare moments of camaraderie, Nevets and Mot talked it over in the bar of their latest crappy motel.

"I don't know about you, Tom," said Nevets, "but I've about had it up to my eyeballs with this case."

(*Weef!*) "You and me both, Steve. All we're doing is chasing one blind lead after another. This case makes the piranhas look good." (*Weef!*) "Just kidding, just kidding," added Mot quickly.

"I've been thinking that maybe we need to try another approach," said Nevets, waving to the waiter to refresh their drinks. "Maybe what we need to do is to try to put ourselves in the place of people looking to buy a human skull. You know, we should do some Internet sleuthing, see what's for sale on eBay, and check out the traffic on skinhead, Goth, and other weirdo blogs. Who knows, our black market skull dealer just might *come to us* if we let it be known online that we're in the market for a couple of noggins."

"Come to us!" (*Weef!*) "Man, I like the sound of that," said Mot.

"OK," said Nevets, "here's the way I suggest we approach this. I'll take all of the Goth, skinhead, and occult sites. You start searching eBay, Craigslist, and other online auction sites. Also, be sure to check out any websites for upstate New York and New England flea markets. Sometimes you see seriously weird stuff for sale at flea markets."

"Got it," said Mot.

Nevets continued, "Now listen, we're going to need aliases in order to do a bunch of web searches without blowing our real identities. Hackers and code-breakers are everywhere on the Internet these days. Who do you want your online persona to be?"

"Whoa! My 'online persona'!" (*Weef! Weef!*) "That's *hot*! Wait 'til I get home and tell Shirley that I've got an online persona." (*Weef!*) "She won't be able to keep her hands off me."

"Get a grip, will you, Tom?" said Nevets, who once again found himself calculating the days until retirement.

"OK. So, who do I want my online persona to be?" (*Weef!*) mused Mot, cupping his chin and wrinkling his mutilated nose as he pondered the question. "How about 'Elliot Ness'?"

"Good God, Tom!" said Nevets. "You can't go online as 'Eliot Ness'! Even stoners will know that's a name only a G-man would use."

"But wait, wait! Listen carefully. I'm deliberately" – (*Weef!*) – "misspelling the first name, see? I'm calling myself 'Elliot' instead of 'Eliot.' That should fool them, don't you think?" (*Weef!*)

Nevets sighed and let his head sag down to his chest. "Tom, Tom...," he began, but then couldn't finish the sentence.

"Still no good, huh?" said Mot in response to Nevets's

headshake.

"I'd say 'no,'" said Nevets. "You might as well call yourself 'J. Edgar's Little Black Dress'! Try again."

"OK then, what about 'Captain Kidd.'" (*Weef!*)

"'Captain Kidd'?" said Nevets. "Where did you get that?"

"Well," (*Weef!*) "it's simple really," said Mot, pleased that he had stumped his better-educated partner. "Captain Kidd was a pirate, right? And pirates always flew a *skull*-and-crossbones flag, right? What do you think?" (*Weef!*)

"Yeah, OK," said Nevets. "That's not bad. Go with it. Me? I think I'll be 'Yorick.'"

"Who the nose-whistling hell is Yorick?" asked Mot.

"Damn, Tom," said Nevets. "Didn't they teach you anything up at the state college? Yorick is the dead court jester in one of Shakespeare's plays. They dig up his skull and somebody says, 'Hey, I knew that poor bastard,' or something like that."

"Oh, *that* Yorick!" said Mot, with an eye-roll. "I thought you meant the League of Legends Yorick. No wonder I was confused. Well, you go right ahead and adopt any old Yorick you want as your alias, Stevie Boy. I'm happy as a pirate."

"OK, Tom. Well, I don't know about you, but I've about had it for today. Tomorrow we'll take a break from interviewing morticians and take 'Captain Kidd' and 'Yorick' for a stroll online. See you at breakfast."

~ ~ ~

The next morning, the two agents sat down at the table in Nevets' room and fired up their trusty government-issue laptops. For a while they surfed the web and blogged in silence. Mot had the brilliant idea to search Google for "bonehead," but all he came up with was a restaurant chain, a company that made helmets for Harley-Davidson fans, and a Danish band that appeared to specialize in heavy metal music. Nevets had the same sort of inspiration and Googled "Yorick," but he backed out of the search quickly when his click on "images" brought up a mixture of fantasy creatures and scantily clad teenagers. He hoped the NSA wasn't monitoring his web browsing too closely.

"Hey, Tom. What did you say yesterday about Yorick

and the league of something?" asked Nevets after shifting over to the PBS website.

"The League of Legends is an online game that my son plays," said Mot. "One of the characters is a humanlike creature named Yorick, a big, ugly dude with eyes that glow. I've been trying to break the kid's gaming habit, but he loves that stuff. He'll sit for hours with his eyes glued to the computer. Why do you ask?"

"I was just looking at the images you get when you search for "Yorick," said Nevets. "Your ugly dude is there along with some other stuff – pretty disturbing, if you don't mind me saying so. If I were you, I'd get the kid off that game ASAP. You having any luck with your searches?"

"Not much," muttered Mot. "I searched for 'pirates' and got baseball sites and lots with information about Johnny Depp. Then I searched for 'bonehead' and got motorcycle helmets and Goth rock, or at least, I think that's what it was. I posted a couple of 'want to buy' notes on skull collectors' blogs, but so far, no response. I think I'll check email."

Two clicks and a password later, and Tom was perusing his latest messages. There was the usual anonymous set of penis enlargement offers and new "selfie at the mall" postings by his Facebook friends. But one message in his inbox caught his attention. It was from someone named SGM and it read as follows:

> FROM: Director, bestheadsforsale.com
> TO: Captainkidd@gmail.com
> SUBJECT: "Searching for..."
> Dear Captain:
> I may be able to help you start your skull collection. Send me your phone # by return email and I'll be in touch. FYI, because I'm concerned that this email account has been hacked, I will be changing accounts in 24 hours. If you are going to respond to this mailbox, do so promptly.
> Sincerely,
> SGM

CHAPTER NINE

Baz Rathbone had definitely been happier. On the one hand, business at PWADS was going like gangbusters. It seemed like old farts were dropping off their perches at a record pace. Baz had done three "cremations/skull sales" in the past week alone and thanks to insider information from his on and off girlfriend Ida Jane, one of the county's visiting nurses, he knew for a fact that a half dozen other local senior citizens were barely clinging to life. Sometimes Baz was amused to think how ridiculously easy it was to make a living off of death.

But if he was pleased with the rate at which people were seeking his after-death services for the obsessively thrifty, Baz was deeply unhappy with the current state of his personal fortune. You see, he had been foolish enough to spend a few days at the Akwesasne Mohawk Casino up near the Canadian border and during that little visit he'd lost his proverbial shirt. And it wasn't just a temporary cash flow problem that Baz was facing. Rather, it came closer to a complete loss of fortune. He had gambled away all of the cash he'd taken with him to the casino, then more money pulled from the ATMs that were conveniently situated throughout the gambling hall, and then cash advances drawn on his American Express, Visa, and Master Card accounts. He was too poor to buy a new shirt, but more importantly, he was too poor to pay either the monthly installment on his new backhoe (kept at the farm for burying those unwanted headless cadavers) or the rent on his PWADS office.

"Dammit!" Baz muttered to himself. "Why wasn't I smart enough to cut my losses and get out when things started to go bad? But, noooo, just like poor old Rollie, I kept saying, 'Today I'm gonna get well!' until I was so skunked I had to sneak off without paying my room bill. Damnation! I hope those Mohawks never track me down. I'll bet they're some kind of pissed off at me." (Note: the aforementioned Rollie was one of Baz's pals from the Navy who had the curious last name of Bugg.)

Baz had borrowed a few hundred dollars from Ida Jane to make it to the end of the month, but he desperately needed to make some money. Which explains, of course, why he'd gotten a little sloppy on the Internet with the customer who styled himself 'Captain Kidd' and why he was contemplating some serious thievery to secure an ape skull for a yo-yo who called himself 'McHead-Case.' "I should just walk away from both of these contacts," thought Baz. But he couldn't quite bring himself to do so.

The "Captain Kidd" thing just smelled wrong to Baz. In a blog on www.youcannotowntoomanyskulls.com, the writer had expressed interest in buying "a standard issue human skull." "Standard issue?" If that didn't have the military or the federal government (both bad news in Baz's opinion) written all over it, he didn't know what did. But did he immediately hit the delete button like he should have? Noooo! He'd responded to the blog post and thereby possibly given some clever computer jock a digital connection right back to his office computer. He should [a] get rid of that computer and [b] move his business. But at the moment, he could afford to do neither. Shit! Sometimes he was his own worst enemy.

But then again, he thought – as the optimistic devil on one shoulder overcame the pessimistic devil on the other – perhaps Captain Kidd was legit. Not only that, but he could be both legit *and* gullible. Might it be possible to dupe the guy into paying twice a skull's going rate, or even more? Even a modest swindle would help until Baz could get his financial feet back under him.

Such was the reasoning that had led Baz to respond to Captain Kidd and to start the process of making phone contact. The guy had one more day to send an email response before Baz canceled his current Gmail account and opened another.

The ape project was a different matter altogether and much safer, or so it seemed to Baz. In the course of establishing his black market bone business, Baz had managed to make contact with a fairly wide network of shadowy characters. It was usually a case of a guy knowing a guy who knew another guy. In this particular instance, Baz's criminal network had chanced to include a Southlands Zoo groundskeeper named McNutt who had heard that Clyde the orang was going to be trucked to New England where he would be stuffed for display. When the line of "guys" finally put McNutt in direct contact with Baz, the former suggested that for a fee he could intercept the truck transporting Clyde to the taxidermist and take possession of the body. Nobody would get hurt, McNutt assured Baz. It could all be done in the dead of night with no confrontation at all. Then the ape's carcass would be rerouted to Baz at a location of the mortician's choosing. Money – cash, please – would change hands and that was that. Nothing could be easier. Given the "critically endangered" status of orangutans in the wild and the resulting ban on all sales of real orangutan skeletal material, Baz felt he could charge McHead-Case upwards of $10,000 for the skull alone. They could dicker about the price over the phone and if the guy cheaped out, well, there had to be lots of other collectors out there who would be happy to pay full price. And what about the ape's post-cranial skeleton? You could rest assured that in this case Baz would make an exception to his normal policy of post-cranial disposal and prepare and sell every last piece of the orang. Yes siree, that one carcass could go a long way toward returning him to financial stability.

~ ~ ~

The very next day, Baz received a phone call at his office that effectively derailed the orangutan project for several weeks and also prompted him to close out all of the current channels by which he could be contacted, i.e., telephone, PO box, email accounts, etc. It hacked him off to have to do this because, among other things, it meant severing communication with this Captain Kidd person just as Baz had decided to do business. Oh well, it couldn't be helped. He could always re-establish contact with Captain Kidd when things cooled down.

The disturbing phone call to the PWADS office was from Sylvester Quinn, the head of Rankin, New York's Better Business Bureau. His conversation with Baz went like this: "Hey, Baz! This is Sly Quinn, over at the BBB. How are you doing this beautiful morning? I haven't seen you at Rotary lately. You been sick or something?"

"Hi, Sly," said Baz, thinking that no good could come of this call. "Nah, I'm fine. My schedule has just been crazy lately, that's all. I'll be back at the club next month for sure. What's up?"

"Listen, Baz, I was reminded just the other day that you've never registered PWADS with the BBB and I'm calling to see if you're ready to sign on." (Irritatingly, Quinn mispronounced the acronym as 'pee-wads,' instead of just 'wads.' Baz bit the end of his tongue to keep from making an acerbic comment.)

"It could do your business a world of good," continued Quinn. "Lots of people check with the BBB before they give a firm their patronage. What do you say?"

"You know, Sly, you could be right," said Baz. "I'll give the matter some serious thought. But just out of curiosity, what was it that reminded you of PWADS in the first place?"

"Well, it was interesting," said Quinn, his voice relaxing now that his enrollment pitch was over. "My secretary got a phone call on Tuesday from an FBI agent named Blot, or something like that, who wanted to know if the Rankin BBB list included any morticians. Suzie took a quick look at our membership list, found no morticians, and told the guy 'no.' That was the end of it, but when she told me about it at the end of the day, I thought, 'Now there's a missed opportunity that old Baz Rathbone will probably want to correct.' Hence, this call."

In the course of Quinn's last comments, Baz had sagged into the overstuffed chair behind his desk. Although the BBB director had no way to know it, Baz had broken out in a cold sweat. His voice had just the slightest tremor as he continued the exchange. "Well now, isn't that the weirdest thing ever? I wonder what an FBI agent is doing looking for morticians? Maybe the Bureau has finally found Jimmy Hoffa and wants a professional to examine the body! That'd be a hoot, don't you think? Anyway, you're absolutely right when you say this is a good reminder for me to sign up with you folks. I'll be down to see you in a couple of days, OK?"

"Hey, that's great, Baz!" said Quinn. "You won't regret it. If I'm not in the office when you swing by, Suzie can help you with the necessary paperwork. Well, I won't take any more of your valuable time. See you at Rotary. Bye-bye."

"Right, bye-bye to you too, Sly," said Baz, who was beginning to feel a little loose in the bowels.

As soon as he put the phone down, Baz went to his storage closet and pulled out a stack of neatly flattened boxes. Then he began to pack the contents of his office. He had been through this drill before, but it was always a pain in the ass. Tomorrow he would put a 'Closed' sign in the window, hop in his car, and drive over to Vermont. With any luck, he could find a nice little town somewhere north of Montpelier that had no resident morticians and a nice bit of secluded property for sale where he could park his RV and dispose of a few headless bodies. It was annoying that he would have to take his new backhoe back to the dealer – the return would no doubt cost him money he didn't have – but he could always buy another. Convicts can't easily buy backhoes, and avoiding becoming a convict was the primary thing on Percy Sanders' mind at the moment.

~ ~ ~

After only a half-day's search in the mountains of far northern Vermont, Baz/Percy hit pay dirt. The tiny town of Upper Gooseberry was nestled in a picturesque cove just north of Mt. Mansfield. Its Main Street was only three blocks long, but it boasted a handful of stores selling Vermont Crafts, a coffee shop with the same name as the town, a general store that carried everything under the sun, and a restaurant called The Country Maid (New Englanders aren't very creative when it comes to naming restaurants). Baz saw lots of the local yokels walking briskly around downtown (it was still pretty cold), and he was pleased to note that their eyes didn't seem to be aglow with intelligence.

By the end of the day, Baz had lied his head off to Ida

Jane and talked her into loaning him yet more money, several thousand dollars this time. He had used part of it to rent a small storefront space on the corner of Main and Brown – giving the realtor another one of his aliases, Bart Zuber – and he had identified some half dozen properties to investigate as potential home sites. One was a tumbledown cabin alongside a pathetically small stream improbably named Roaring Goose Creek. The house was a real "handy man's special," but it came with twelve acres of very secluded land at the end of a private dirt road. Baz figured he would devote the next morning to looking at other properties, but if nothing superior to Roaring Goose Creek had turned up by lunchtime, he'd begin the purchase arrangements for the cabin and land. Then it would be back to Rankin and the mad scramble to move his home and business to more of an "FBI free" neck of the woods. The things a man had to do these days just to make a living!

CHAPTER TEN

The moment Lazlo Wetzo arrived at work on that Monday morning, he knew there was something different, something very nicely different, about the mortuary. The lingering smell of embalming fluids had been replaced by a delicious feminine fragrance. As he walked past the displays of caskets and urns on the way to his tiny office, Ron Styx gave a yell. "Hey, Laz! Come here a minute will you? I want you to meet someone."

Lazlo took a left turn into his boss's office and as he walked into the room his heart skipped a beat. One of the young women that he and Uli had ogled so outrageously at the Country Girl Diner was sitting opposite Mr. Styx. "Oh crap!" thought Lazlo. "She's tracked me down and made some sort of sexual harassment complaint. Now I'm in for it!"

"Annette Fibrowski, meet Lazlo Wetzo," said Ron, who showed no outward sign of being annoyed. "Laz started working as my assistant mortician back in January and he's made great progress learning the tricks of the trade. He'll be able to teach you quite a bit, Annette. Laz, Annette here is a senior up at Fort Kent and she'll be interning with us for the next six months. She's majoring in gerontology and has two minors, psychology and social work. Annette thinks she would like to devote her career to working with bereaved senior citizens. Six months with us will let her test the waters of the funeral industry, so to speak."

"Uh, hi," said Lazlo, extending his hand. "Welcome to Styx's."

"Thanks," said Annette, whose face had spread into a mischievous grin. "I'm glad to see you've gotten those eyes fixed. Back in their sockets, I mean."

"Oh, yeah, I guess we were a bit obvious the other night, huh?" said Lazlo. "Sorry about that."

"Do you two already know each other?" asked Ron.

"Well, not exactly," said Annette with a light laugh. "I was in the Country Girl with a sorority sister the other night and Lazlo and a friend of his were giving us a serious once-over from across the room. I wish guys knew how silly they look with their jaws unhinged and their eyes popped out. Jenny and I wrote them off as Grade A losers and took off. But I've got to say, Lazlo, you look very nearly human with your face rearranged." Then once again she laughed that musical laugh of hers. ("I could take verbal abuse from this woman all day long," Lazlo thought to himself.)

"I hope Laz didn't misbehave so badly that you feel like you can't work with him, Annette," said Ron. "Since I have to travel to the other Styx's mortuaries pretty regularly, the best set-up for an internship would be for you two to team up."

"No, no, don't worry about that," said Annette quickly. "I'm sure we'll be just fine. Guys will be guys, especially when they travel in pairs or, worse yet, in packs. I can tell from Lazlo's hangdog expression that he's properly embarrassed about the whole thing now that he's been called out. We're good. Right, Lazlo?"

"Absolutely," said Lazlo. "I'll be happy to show you how things work around here and to have your help for a few months. I'm sure you can teach me a lot about dealing with old folks in crisis. And again, I apologize for the other night."

"Apology accepted," said Annette brightly. "Shall I call you Lazlo or Laz?"

"Laz would be great, thanks. How about you? Annette or just Ann?"

"My pals call me 'A-Fib,'" she said, yet again filling the room with her wonderful laughter. "Just don't use it in a doctor's office or hospital."

"Cool!" said Laz, as both he and Ron broke into laughter. "What a great nickname! 'A-Fib' it is then. When do you want to start? We have a client coming in at ten to make arrangements for his late wife, if today's good for you."

"You bet it is," said Annette, her voice betraying her excitement. "Do you have a ladies room where I can freshen up a bit? I'd like to look as professional as I can."

~ ~ ~

Happily for all concerned, Annette proved to be a natural for the funeral business. She had no problem working around dead bodies and soon knew enough anatomy to help with the embalming procedures. Additionally, she was a sympathetic listener and thus excellent at dealing with bereaved customers, whose confidence she gained almost immediately. And, it must be said, her stunning good looks brightened up Styx's Riverside Mortuary wonderfully. She gave the place new life, even if she couldn't quite manage to bring the dead back to life.

It wasn't long before Lazlo fairly worshipped the ground Annette walked on. Not only was she gorgeous, she was also super smart and had a wicked sense of humor. She assimilated the embalming room procedures with record speed, and likewise the details of the different mortuary packages that Styx's offered its customers. Lazlo had to remind himself repeatedly that he was the mentor and she was the trainee.

Of course, there was the minor problem of Annette being a good three inches taller than Lazlo, but they were too busy working together and having fun together to worry about that. Pretty soon, each was appreciating the other as something more than a colleague.

About two weeks after Annette had begun her internship at Styx's, a small woman of singular appearance walked through the mortuary's front door. She wore a red mackinaw coat and a matching plaid cap complete with earflaps, and she had a look in her eyes that was somewhere between dreamy and mad as a March hare. Lazlo thought she was probably in her mid-fifties, but that was just a wild guess. Annette happened to be sitting at the front desk when the woman arrived and therefore was the first to speak to her.

"Hello and welcome to Styx's Riverside Mortuary. My name is Annette Fibrowski. How can we help you?"

"My name is Marcie Hampstead and my husband has just passed away and left me all alone in this cruel world. I've come to make his final arrangements."

"Oh, Mrs. Hampstead," said Annette, coming from

behind the desk and putting her arm around the woman's shoulders. "I am so sorry to hear about your husband. What was his name?"

"His name was Pierre Seamus Angus Hampstead and his grandparents were French, Irish, Scottish, and English. But I didn't call him by any of those names. I just called him my Little Pickle Pie. That's the name I'd like to have engraved on his urn, if possible."

"I'm sure that can be arranged, Mrs. Hampstead. But what an unusual nickname you had for your Pierre. May I ask where it came from?"

"Well, you see," said Mrs. Hampstead, coloring slightly, "Pierre had a cute, but very short pickle and... Are you all right, honey?" she asked in response to Annette's violent coughing attack. Now it was the older woman's turn to lend a comforting arm.

(Gasp! Choke!) "Yes, yes, I'm fine, thanks. You know how those sudden tickles in your throat can make you cough." (Hack!) "Anyway, I'm sure we can accommodate your requests for your husband, pretty much regardless of what they may be."

"I'm so glad to hear you say that, honey," said Mrs. Hampstead, "because they may be a little different from what you're used to."

And that proved to be the case in spades. When Mrs. Hampstead explained to Ron, Lazlo, and Annette just how she wanted Pierre's remains to be dealt with, Ron had to admit that her wishes were unique in his many years of experience as a mortician. He thought *maybe* Styx's could fulfill them, but, as he told the grieving widow, in order to be absolutely sure, he needed to check with the mortuary's lawyer that everything was legal and also with a local taxidermist for advice about procedures. In a nutshell, Marcie Hampstead wanted Styx's to stuff her Little Pickle Pie so she could put him on display in her family room.

"Let me get this straight, mam," said Lazlo in disbelief. "You want us to prepare your late husband's body so he can *go on display* in your home?"

"That's right, sweetie. Mr. Wetzo, did you say your name

was? My goodness, what an unusual name that is. Is it Italian? Lots of Italian names end in vowels, you know. No? Hungarian, you say. That's interesting. Anyway, I want my dear Pierre's entire body, every last little pickle bit of it" (here Annette had another coughing fit) "to be preserved for ever and ever, just like those wonderful animals one sees in museums. So, just like those animals, I want to have him stuffed. I want him arranged in a reclining pose with his legs stretched out and his hands clasped over his tummy, and I want him dressed in his jeans, flannel shirt, and sheepskin slippers. I plan to put him in his La-Z-Boy recliner in front of the big screen TV he loved so much and keep him with me until it's time to stuff me too."

"OK," said Lazlo, trying to sound nonchalant, when in fact he was utterly stunned. "Uh, well, maybe we can do all that for you, but like Mr. Styx says, we'll need to check on the legality of stuffing a human being and – assuming the lawyers give us the go-ahead – call in an expert in the science of taxidermy. Do you know Uliba Helmsman, Mrs. Hampstead? He has a shop just outside of town."

"Well, no, I don't believe I do. 'Uliba' is his first name, did you say? Now that's *got* to be Italian. It sounds strange *and* it ends in a vowel. But why do you need to talk to him? This isn't going to raise the price of preserving poor dear Pierre, is it? I mean, I had some surgery done a few years ago and got billed for some 'assisting surgeon' who I didn't know and never asked for. Please tell me this isn't like that."

"No, no, Mrs. Hampstead...Marcie," said Ron, sitting down beside her and patting her arm. "Uliba will just give us expert advice on the correct stuffing procedures. I guarantee you that you won't be charged for the consultation. We just want to be sure that Pierre is given the best preparation that modern mortuary and taxidermy sciences can provide."

"OK, well, I believe you, Mr. Styx. Everything that I've ever heard is that you run a very professional and up-and-up business here. So, when can the four of us get together with Mr. Helmsman? I'd like to move forward with Pierre's arrangements as soon as possible because I hate the thought of him lying in a cold storage unit. It sounds so uncomfortable."

As luck would have it, at that very instant Uli Helmsman stuck his head through the door of Styx's Riverside Mortuary and gave a shout: "Hey, Laz. You and the beautiful A-Fib ready to go to lunch?"

"And as if by magic, here's our taxidermist," said Lazlo, who excused himself, went to the mortuary's reception area, and retrieved Uli. As they walked back down the hall, Laz explained the unusual request that confronted them.

"This lady wants to have her husband stuffed, Uli, so she can lay him out in a recliner and stare at him for the rest of her life. Weirdest thing I've ever heard of, but there it is. We told her we'd need to talk to a professional taxidermist to see if it was possible and right on cue, here you are." Rounding the corner into the conference room, Lazlo said, "Mrs. Marcie Hampstead, this is Uliba Helmsman, Moose Wallow's local taxidermist."

"My goodness, you're a big boy, aren't you?" said Mrs. Hampstead as she gave Uli the once-over. "I didn't think Italians ever got as big as you. I expect it's from eating lots of seafood, drinking red wine, and living a clean life." Lazlo choked back a laugh at the "clean life" comment.

"No, I'm not Italian, I'm afraid, Mrs. Hampstead. I'm just a Scotch-Irish mongrel from North Carolina and I prefer a nice steak to seafood. But look here, Lazlo tells me that you want your husband to be stuffed. I'm not so sure that's legal in Maine, but it's worth running by a lawyer. State laws do specify that a dead person's written instructions concerning corpse disposal are legally binding on the person or persons responsible for funeral arrangements. So if your husband left a written request to be preserved through taxidermy, you might be on solid legal grounds. But I should tell you that stuffing your husband might not turn out to be such a good decision in the long run. Have you ever heard of Jeremy Bentham?"

"No, dear, I don't believe I have," replied Mrs. Hampstead. "Does he live in Moose Wallow?"

"No, mam," said Uli. "He was a famous philosopher who lived in England back a couple of hundred years ago. The reason I mention him is that, following his wishes, he was stuffed when he died and then put on public display. Everything went fine for a while, but then, as I understand it, his head started to go bad. First the scalp puckered up and the face got all taut. Then the whole thing turned 'cheesy,' for lack of a better term. In the end, they had to substitute a wax replica for poor old Jeremy's head."

"Oh my, how awful!" sputtered Mrs. Hampstead. "I don't want that for my Little Pickle Pie. What do you suggest?"

"Well, mam, what I would like to do if we go down the taxidermy road – and I apologize if this sounds too grisly – is get your permission to detach your husband's head from his body so we can replace his actual scalp and face with a nice plastic death mask. No one will ever know the difference once the head and body are put back together. This way, if Pierre's head needs touch-up work down the road, we can simply borrow the skull for a few days and then get it right back to you. I'll bet Ron here can even come up with a long-term maintenance plan to cover the cost of regular inspections and touch-ups if they're needed. What do you say?"

"Oh dear," said Mrs. Hampstead. "Take his head off, you say? Replace the skin with plastic and then screw his head back on, so to speak? Well, uh, I guess that's OK, if that's your best advice. You folks are the professionals, after all. And besides, Little Pickle Pie will never know, will he? I mean, he's in Heaven, probably chatting with God right now. OK, let's do exactly as you say, Mr. Helmsman. Mr. Styx, can you put all of this down in a contract for me to sign? I can come back sometime tomorrow if that's enough time to write it up."

"Give me until tomorrow afternoon to run all this by the legal beagles, Marcie. If they say 'no problem,' I'll be pleased to draw up the necessary papers," said Ron, giving Mrs. Hampstead's arm another pat. Then he helped her to her car in the lot out back, leaving Annette, Lazlo, and Uli looking at each other and shaking their heads in disbelief.

~ ~ ~

As it turned out, Mrs. Hampstead's mortuary request

was *not* legal in Maine or anywhere else in the United States. Ron Styx got an absolutely unequivocal ruling to that effect from his lawyer. The day after her visit to the funeral home, Marcie was disappointed to learn that she couldn't have Pierre stuffed, but she found some consolation in the prospect of having his sweet face preserved as a death mask. Besides, she was enjoying the brouhaha resulting from her original plans for Little Pickle Pie. Right after the meeting at Styx's, Marcie had run into her nephew, a reporter for the local paper, *The Daily Wallow*, and even though she'd known the legal questions had not been resolved, Marcie had outlined her elaborate plans for Pierre Seamus Angus Hampstead's preservation and display. Recognizing a good story when it was handed to him, the nephew went straight to the office and wrote it up for the next morning's paper. So before Ron Styx could tell her that it was off, the entire town of Moose Wallow was led to believe that Pierre's stuffing/death masking/La-Z-Boy displaying was on. The newspaper piece even included Marcie's plans to throw a big homecoming party in Pierre's honor once he was "done." "He's gonna look beautiful," she had told her nephew. "Everyone is going to want to see him." The article drew a lot of interest, including that of FBI agents Steven Nevets and Tom Mot, who read the story in their motel rooms in upstate Vermont.

CHAPTER ELEVEN

Once the news story broke about the planned mortuary arrangements for P. S. A. Hampstead, it instantly went viral. (For the record, despite his suspicious sounding initials, Pierre's prostate had nothing to do with his death.) Newspapers spread the story, first across New England and then around the world, as did dozens of Internet blogs. Marcie Hampstead was bombarded by offers from videographers who wanted to film Pierre's preservation and homecoming party, and then upload the video to YouTube. Even the checkout-line tabloids got into the act, with several featuring stories about Little Pickle Pie, and one publishing a cover photo that claimed to show a stuffed Pierre sitting on the lap of one of the Kardashians. Recipes for pickle pies began to show up on all of the TV cooking shows. The follow-up note that stuffing Pierre had been determined to be illegal did nothing to stop the tidal wave of the original story.

Norman McLaughlin read the news story as he sat in the kitchen of his skull-filled farmhouse north of Bangor. He asked both Red Skelton the cat and Bill Grogan the goat what they thought of it, but both animals were noncommittal. For his part, Norman was hugely excited – almost obscenely so – about the idea of acquiring a stuffed person for his collection. He considered sending an email to the shadowy SGM asking about the possibility of such a purchase, but then he thought better of it. Even more than a stuffed person, Norman wanted an ape skull and SGM had said he was very close to obtaining one. Yes, it was probably best not to confuse his wish list with SGM unnecessarily. It would be one thing if he (Norman) could afford both items, but he couldn't. Still, he thought it wouldn't hurt to get in touch with this Hampstead woman to offer his condolences and inquire about making a pilgrimage to see her husband's remains. And also, since the newspaper piece had included the names of the mortician and taxidermist in charge of Pierre's preservation, he could send congratulatory notes to the artists whose work would soon beautify Mrs. Hampstead's family room. After all, thought Norm, "I might need to avail myself of their services one of these days." He was thinking of his great-aunt Lucille, who was nearly ninety. Norman was her closest living kin and Aunt Lucy was loopy enough to make him think he could easily get her signature on a document requesting post-mortem stuffing and subsequent display at her nephew's house. He sat down at the computer and after just a few minutes of searching, he had found email addresses for both Lazlo Wetzo and Uli Helmsman. "What very strange names they have up in the north woods," thought Norman as he began this message:

> FROM: Norman McLaughlin <McHead-Case@gmail.com>
> TO: Lazlo Wetzo <assmortician@styxsriversidemortuary.com>, Uli Helmsman <Uli@moosewallowwildlife.com>
> SUBJECT: Hampstead preservation
> Dear Mr. Wetzo and Mr. Helmsman:
> I am a collector of osteological and other after-death memorabilia and I have just read the newspaper account of your remarkable plans to preserve Mr. Pierre S. A. Hampstead. The case seems to be truly unique in my experience and I would love the chance to meet with you and discuss it. I am writing simultaneously to Mrs. Hampstead and if she grants me permission to visit once her husband's body has been completed and is on display at her home, I would love to drop by your places of business at the same time. I live just a little over three hours away down near Bangor.
> I look forward to hearing from you. In the meantime, I want to offer my very sincere congratulations on Mr. Pierre Hampstead's preservation. I think it will break new ground in the science of post-mortem treatment.

Sincerely,
Norman McLaughlin

After emailing Lazlo and Uli, Norman composed a handwritten note of condolence to Mrs. Marcie Hampstead, whose address he found in the Moose Wallow white pages. In his note, Norm begged permission to visit Mrs. Hampstead sometime later in the summer in order to pay his respects to her husband. He buttered her up by saying he had no doubt that her treatment of Pierre would set a new trend in after-death procedures. No longer would people be limited to the traditional mortuary methods of burial, cremation, or even cryostasis. Thanks to her, the taxidermic preservation of humans was about to become a commonplace event in America. He included all of his contact information – postal address, email address, telephone number – at the end of his note and asked Mrs. Hampstead to please get back to him concerning a visit.

And finally, Norman couldn't resist sending a brief email to SGM, asking if he had seen the various reports on Pierre Hampstead and inquiring what SGM thought about the case. As it happened, SGM was just as intrigued as Norman by the Hampstead story, but he was also very wary. He was always wary of anything that brought attention to the mortuary business. Too much attention from the wrong sort of people could lead to the discovery of bottom-feeders like Baz Rathbone.

~ ~ ~

A-Fib was at her usual station behind the reception desk at Styx's when agents Nevets and Mot walked through the door. Her first impression was that they were salesmen of some sort, either that or very old Mormons still out proselytizing. Whoever they were, it was her job to be welcoming and so she gave them a cheerful greeting. "Hello and welcome to Styx's Riverside Mortuary. My name is Annette Fibrowski. How may I help you today?"

"Hello, Ms. Fibrowski," said Nevets, stepping forward with his badge open for Annette's inspection. "I am Special Agent Steven Nevets and this is Agent Tom Mot. We work out of the Boston Field Office of the FBI."

"Holy moly!" said A-Fib, her eyes widening and jaw dropping. "FBI agents? What's going on? Who do you want to speak to? Mr. Styx, the owner of the mortuary, is out of town visiting one of the other branches, but Lazlo Wetzo, Mr. Styx's assistant, is here. Do you want me to go get Lazlo?"

"It would be very helpful if you would do that," said Nevets. "We're very anxious to meet Mr. Wetzo. Is there a room where we can all sit down and talk? We'd like to have you there too."

"Yeah, sure," said A-Fib. "The conference room is right down here. Come make yourselves at home while I get Lazlo."

A-Fib found Lazlo in the embalming room finishing his monthly inventory of fluids and equipment. She scurried over to him and said in an urgent whisper, "Hey Laz, the feds are here to talk to you. What the hell have you been up to? If I need to cover for you, I will, but I need to know what's going on before I say something stupid."

"Huh?" said Lazlo, clearly having trouble processing what Annette was saying. "Feds? What feds? I have no earthly idea what you are talking about."

"Well, my lad," said Annette, "two beefy FBI agents in tan trench coats are waiting for you in the conference room. You and Uli haven't been selling weed around town, have you? No? Well, something sure has drawn the law's attention. Anyway, look sharp because they said they're anxious to meet you."

Feeling pretty anxious himself – although he wasn't sure why – Lazlo followed Annette back down the hall to the conference room where she introduced him to Nevets and Mot. The four of them sat down at the table, the agents looking cocksure and suspicious, and the young folks looking nervous. Nevets took a newspaper from his briefcase and opened it to what looked to be a well-thumbed article. Mot opened his laptop computer and prepared to take notes.

"First of all," said Nevets, "I should tell you that this isn't a criminal investigation..."

"Yet," (*Weef!*) said Mot without looking up. His whistling

nose drew a startled look from Annette.

"Now, Tom," said Nevets as he gave his partner a "tut tut" look. "We don't want to be too scary. No point in that. What I was about to say is that you are not under suspicion of committing a crime, so we're not going to read you your Miranda rights or anything like that. In fact, we've come seeking your help. We're here hoping you can assist us with an investigation that's centered over in New York State."

Lazlo could feel his heart playing the conga drums inside his chest and he just hoped to God that he didn't keel over in a cataplectic fit. "Well," he finally managed to say, although in a voice about three octaves higher than normal, "uh, we'd be happy to help in any way we can. Just tell us what this is about." ("Breathe deeply, Lazlo," he thought to himself.)

"Sure, that's fair," said Nevets. "OK, for the past several weeks, we've been interviewing morticians doing business in upstate New York in connection with a possible case of fraud compounded by corpse abuse. Specifically, we have a complaint from a woman in Boston who claims to have seen her late husband's skull in the possession of a skinhead with whom she was having a one-night stand. This surprised her – seeing the skull, that is, not having a one-night stand – since she had paid for the skull to be cremated along with the rest of his body – her husband's body, that is, not the skinhead's. The woman's story is a little confusing because she has a long-standing drug problem and therefore is not as reliable an informant as we might wish..."

"She a flipping meth head," (*Weef!*) "that's" (*Weef!*) "what she is," said Mot, as he typed away on his computer. (Annette was now peering closely at Mot's mutilated nose. "That thing's a mess," she thought to herself.)

"Now, Tom, that's not the kindest characterization in the world," said Nevets, shaking his head, "but not far off the mark, I suppose. Not only is our informant's memory of her husband's death and alleged cremation a bit fuzzy, but she also lacks any documentation about the funeral arrangements. Still, her husband's cranium had a very distinctive feature – a bone flap shaped like the state of Texas – and she swears the skull the skinhead was using as a candlestand was similarly marked. Anyway, when she asked the man how he came to possess her husband's skull, he became aggressive and she fled. When the Boston police went searching for him a few days later, he was gone without a trace."

Lazlo thought he'd gotten the gist of Nevets's story, but Annette was confused and asked for clarification. "So let me get this straight," she said. "A female druggie comes to you and claims that, at some point in the past, her husband died and she arranged for him to be cremated – in his *entirety*. Then much later, she saw her husband's skull being used as a candlestand by a skinhead who she'd shacked up with. Is that about right?"

"You've mostly got it right, Ms. Fishkowski," (*Weef!*) said Mot.

"Fibrowski," corrected Annette.

"Sorry," said Mot, in a voice that sounded bored, not apologetic. "Anyway, one additional detail" (*Weef!*) "is that the original report was made to the Boston police, not to us. We got the case because it looks like the skull in question" (*Weef!*) "has probably been illegally transported across several state lines, making it a federal matter." (*Weef! Weef!* Any variant of the phrase, "make a federal case out of it" always excited Mot.)

"So," Mot continued, "we figure we're looking at three crimes. First, there's fraud:" (*Weef!*) "someone took the widow's money and then failed to perform the agreed upon cremation – at least *all* of the agreed upon cremation." (*Weef!*) "Second, there's corpse abuse in that someone removed" (*Weef!*) "the husband's head, cleaned it up, and then probably sold it. Third, there's the illegal interstate transport stuff. So, do either of you know anything about swindles like that being perpetrated by New England morticians?" (*Weef!*)

"Whoa!" said Annette. "Not me. But then I'm just a six-month intern down from U. Maine at Fort Kent. I can tell you one thing, however: in my short time here at Styx's, everything has been on the up-and-up. If bodies come in to be cremated, they get cremated – every last bit of them. If they come in for embalming and burial, that's what they get, and everything, including the skull, goes into the grave. I'm right on all this, aren't I, Lazlo?"

"Yeah, absolutely," said Laz, who had recovered the power of normal speech. "The stuff you guys are describing is bizarre, really grotesque! None of the dozen or so fellow morticians that I've met thus far would ever do anything like that, and certainly not Mr. Styx. He's as honest as the day is long. I mean, we try our very best to be comforting and supportive for the grieving family and friends. Jeez, I can't imagine *anyone* cheating on a cremation contract or selling part of a body! Whoever this person is, I hope you catch him – or her, I suppose – real soon. This sort of thing smears the good name of all morticians, everywhere."

"We keep detailed records of every corpse that comes through the place and of all embalming and cremations," said Annette. "And if Mr. Styx were here, I'm sure he would offer to let you go over them. Right, Lazlo? You can also check our record at the BBB. We've got an A+ rating with no complaints."

"We will definitely need to look over those office records," said Nevets. "I can do that right now, as a matter of fact, while Tom goes over to the BBB office. But listen, we also wanted to ask you about this Marcie Hampstead thing. Mr. Wetzo, were you really planning to help preserve her husband by taxidermy so he could be displayed in their home?"

"That was what she wanted," said Lazlo, "but when Mr. Styx checked into it, he was told preserving a human in that way is illegal. He told Mrs. Hampstead that, but the news story about her original plans had already been published and before we knew it, we were reading about it everywhere. Mr. Hampstead's body is out back, embalmed in the traditional way. Uli Helmsman is going to mold a death mask for the widow before the body is cremated."

"Who is" (*Weef!*) "this Helmsman guy?" asked Mot. "We read about him in the newspaper article. We'll need to talk to him too." (*Weef!*)

"He's a friend of ours," said Lazlo. "A local taxidermist.

That's how he got pulled into the Pierre Hampstead thing. I can take you out to his studio whenever you want."

(*Weef!*) "That'd be good," said Mot. "Probably tomorrow sometime."

"Agent Mot," said Annette, "do you mind if I ask what happened to your nose? It's none of my business, of course, but I've never been able to keep from asking embarrassing questions."

"Well, since you've asked so nicely, I'll tell you," (*Weef!*) said Mot. "We were working a case out on Martha's Vineyard a few years ago and there was a nutcase out there" (*Weef!*) "who kept piranha fish as pets in his house. One of the damn things bit me" (*Weeeeff!*) "on the nose and it's never been the same. Sorry about all the whistling."

"That nutcase's name wouldn't have been Uxem, by any chance, would it?" asked Lazlo.

"I *thought* there was something familiar about your last name!" exclaimed Nevets. "Mike Uxem, the piranha owner, had a friend named Artie Wetzo. Artie wouldn't be related to you, would he, Lazlo?"

"Yeah, he's my uncle," said Laz. "I remember him telling me the story of the FBI guy who got a chunk of his nose chewed off by a fish, but wasn't there something about a self-inflicted gunshot wound as well?"

(*Weeeefff!*) "Never you damn well mind about that," grunted Mot. "The little fish bastard wouldn't let go and so I tried to shoot his ass." (*Weef! Weef!*) "That's all. So you're Artie Wetzo's kin, huh? Does he know you're up here in Maine plotting to stuff people like they were ten-point bucks?"

"Now, Mr. Mot, I explained all that," said Lazlo, feeling his chest tighten and his blood pressure go up. "We listened to Mrs. Hampstead's request, checked into it, and then told her it was illegal. I'm sorry if Annette's question has pissed you off, but there's been no crime committed here at Styx's."

"OK, OK," said Steve Nevets, "let's end the interview for now. I'd like to see those records, if you don't mind, Lazlo. Put in a call to your boss for his permission, if you need to. Ms. Fibrowski, it would be helpful if you showed Agent Mot the whereabouts of the BBB office. And for both of you, let's plan on a trip out to see Mr. Helmsman tomorrow morning, shall we? And please don't call and tell him we're coming. We find it useful at times to have the element of surprise on our side."

CHAPTER TWELVE

Around ten the next morning, a two-vehicle convoy left Styx's Riverside Mortuary and headed out of town toward Uli Helmsman's taxidermy shop. Lazlo and Annette led the way in Laz's old white van; agents Nevets and Mot brought up the rear in their Ford Fiesta. They parked in front of the shop and Lazlo led the way through the main entrance.

"Hey, Uli," shouted Lazlo, "you've got visitors."

From somewhere in the back of the building, Uli yelled back. "Hey, Laz. I'll be there in a minute. I accidently whacked Bookworm Bear with a two-by-four and chipped one of her teeth. I need a couple more minutes for the super glue to set. Help yourself to a joint."

"'Help yourself to a joint,' huh?" (*Weef!*) said Mot, looking very pleasantly surprised. He ambled over to the front counter, looked behind it, and retrieved a coffee mug containing several fat reefers. "Well, well," (*Weef!*) said Mot, "look what we have here."

"What do you think of that shit, Laz?" said Uli, still shouting from the rear of the shop. "That's not ditch week, is it? Only the finest ganja for my guests Lazlo Wetzo and the lovely A-Fib." At that point, the taxidermist emerged from behind a rack of storage shelves and realized that his friends weren't alone.

"Hey there, Lazlo and Annette," said Uli. "Who are these nice folks you've brought with you? A couple of bird hunters, unless I miss my guess."

"Nice try at nonchalance, my friend," (*Weef!*) "but no cigar, marijuana or otherwise," said Mot as he flipped open his badge and displayed it for Uli's inspection. Steve Nevets also pulled out his badge and showed it to the startled taxidermist.

"Well, I'll be damned," said Uli. "FBI agents right here in little old Moose Wallow. What's next, a FEMA prison train running up the old Maine Northern Railway line? It's funny that I didn't hear the black helicopter landing out front. So, what can I say? You've got me dead to rights on pot possession, but since I've only got enough for personal use – and one or two extra joints to offer my friends and visiting narcs – I'm betting you're here for something else."

"You're right, Mr. Helmsman, we're not here about drugs," said Nevets, "although you really should be more careful. The local state police might be real interested in the details of your marijuana stash. Anyway, I think Agent Mot and I will have to turn down your kind offer of a joint, although I can't speak for Lazlo and Annette here."

"None for me," said A-Fib.

"Ditto," said Lazlo.

"But, look here, we're getting off on the wrong foot, Mr. Helmsman – or may I call you Uli?" said Nevets, assuming his good cop persona. "My partner and I are in Maine investigating possible criminal acts by one or more morticians in New York State. We became aware of Lazlo's involvement in the embalming trade through the newspaper article about Mrs. Marcie Hampstead's plans for her late husband – an article that also mentioned you as the expert taxidermy consultant. Anyway, Lazlo has already explained that Mrs. Hampstead's request had to be denied when Mr. Styx's attorneys advised him that it's illegal in Maine to preserve humans using taxidermic techniques. We looked over the embalming and cremation records at Styx's Riverside and everything there seems to be in order."

"When you say 'criminal acts' by some of the New York morticians, exactly what do you mean?" asked Uli, as he tucked the mug full of reefers back under the counter and away from Tom Mot's glare.

"We have reason to believe that there has been at least one act of fraud – specifically, accepting payment for a cremation and then not destroying the entire body – and one act of corpse abuse – specifically, stealing and then selling the skull of the aforementioned individual. Because the corpse abuse charge involves human remains being sold across state lines, the FBI got pulled into a case that would otherwise have gone to the local police," said Nevets.

(*Weef!*) "Damn waste of our time and taxpayers' money," (*Weef!*) muttered Mot under his breath. It had been a long time since he'd attested anybody and he longed to cuff this oversized pothead. He planned to have a word with Nevets over supper to see if they couldn't come up with some workable charge against Uli.

"Huh," said Uli. "Well, I don't know anything about cremation fraud or stolen human skulls. As you can see all around you, I work entirely with animals. Deer, birds, prize fish, you name it. And the only morticians I'm acquainted with are Ron Styx, Lazlo here, and, of course, the lovely A-Fib – although as a college intern, I don't know if she counts in your book."

"So neither you nor Lazlo know anything about a trade in stolen human body parts?" asked Nevets, getting to the heart of the matter.

"Nope, not me," said Uli.

"Ditto," said Lazlo, for the second time in five minutes. But then, thinking over Nevets question, he amended his answer. "But, you know, Uli, there *was* that weird email that we got right after the Hampstead thing went viral. What was the name of the guy who wrote to us? Casey something?"

"Naw, that's not quite right," said Uli. "Wait a minute and I'll find it on my machine." He typed a few strokes into his countertop computer and then swiveled the monitor around for everyone to read. "His name was Norman McLaughlin. His Gmail user name is McHead-Case. That's what you're remembering."

"Yeah, right. McLaughlin, that's it. He was really excited about the Hampstead stuffing thing," said Lazlo. "What does he call himself in the email? A 'collector of osteological and other after-death memorabilia.' So, he's keen on bones and God knows what else. Sounds downright creepy to me, and that's coming from a mortician."

"Tom," said Nevets thoughtfully, "what are the chances that we can use Mr. McLaughlin's email address to take a little look at his Gmail files? You know a lot more about hacking – I mean digital infiltration – than I do."

(*Weef!*) "I think I can send Mr. McLaughlin an imbedded program in a legitimate-looking email that will cause his computer to spill its guts," (*Weef! Weef! Weef!*) said Mot, his whistling nose betraying his excitement at doing something more than interviewing gravediggers. "Of course, I could just check with the NSA in case they've already done the hacking – sorry, infiltrating – for us."

"Yeah, right," scoffed Nevets. "Do you really think those boys at NSA are going to play nicely and share information with two FBI agents? I seriously doubt it. We're on our own out here. So go for it and see what you can learn about Mr. McLaughlin. Who knows what lengths he's willing to go to in order to add to his 'osteological collection.' He could be our skull merchant, for all we know."

"Now, Lazlo, Annette, and Uli," said Nevets, "I hope it goes without saying that you heard none of the exchange I just had with Tom. Equally, it goes without saying that neither Tom nor I saw any evidence of drug use in Uli's taxidermy shop. Are we all in agreement on those points? Does a bit of quid pro quo work for all of you?"

"I'm in," said Lazlo.

"Me too," chirped Annette.

"My lips are sealed," said Uli. "I could use a beer. Anybody else want one? The offer extends to feds too." After making the obligatory "it's kind of early" comments, both Nevets and Mot accepted a brew.

~ ~ ~

Say what you will about Tom Mot, despite being chronically grouchy and showing frequent disfluency, he *was* a skilled computer nerd. In less time than it took a certain CIA director to spill classified beans to his mistress, Mot had done a sweet B&E job on Norman McLaughlin's computer. Among the things Mot found was that Norman had some shady friends who needed looking into. One email contact in particular, a person who signed his emails with the initials 'SGM,' struck Mot as especially suspicious. McLaughlin had emailed SGM just a few days ago asking if he had seen the article on Pierre Hampstead. The tone of the note suggested that McLaughlin longed to add a stuffed person to his after-death memorabilia and hoped that SGM might be able to help with this. Unfortunately, the only SGM Mot could find on the Internet who had – in this case, *had* had – anything to do with bones was Samuel George Morton (1799-1851). The connection to the present case looked promising, however; Samuel George Morton was one of early America's most avid collectors of human *skulls*. The hundreds of skulls that Morton acquired during his lifetime were now housed at the University of Pennsylvania's Penn Museum. "Hmm," thought Mot. "Might be worth a visit."

The other very interesting piece of information that Mot extracted from Norman McLaughlin's computer was the latter's keen desire to add an ape skull to his collection. "Jeez," thought Tom, "this guy's house must smell like hell!"

When Mot shared selected pieces of his digital discoveries with the rest of the gang, Uli was most interested in the part about McLaughlin being anxious to buy an ape skull.

"Go figure!" said Uli. "In a couple of weeks, Lazlo and I are going to take a road trip down south to pick up two bodies: one's a woman to be brought back and buried in the family graveyard here in Maine and the other's an dead orangutan to be stuffed for display at the Southlands Zoo in Charlotte, North Carolina. Weird, huh? Quite a coincidence."

"In our experience," said Nevets, "things that look coincidental often are anything but. How often do ape skulls come available in the U.S.?"

"Real ape skulls, as opposed to plastic replicas? Extremely rarely, I'd say," said Uli. "But are you suggesting somebody, this McLaughlin guy or somebody else, is planning on trying to get his hands on the Southlands ape? How would they do that? And anyway, how would they even know about it?"

"At the moment, I can't answer either of your questions," said Nevets. "But I'd be willing to bet that there's some connection between McLaughlin, his friend SGM, your ape carcass, and an ongoing black market trade in skulls. Well, if you ask me, we've done a good morning's work! It's made me hungry, that's for sure. What about you, Tom?"

(*Weef! Weef!*) His companions took the two nose-whistle blasts from Mot as an affirmative.

"Last night we ate something disgusting called moose turd stew at Ricky's Restaurant up in Fort Kent," continued Nevets. "I'm not about to go back there. Is there a decent restaurant here in Moose Wallow? Someplace where you can get a good burger without worrying about coming down with dysentery?"

"The Country Girl Diner," said Annette, Lazlo, and Uli in unison. "Follow us."

CHAPTER THIRTEEN

After a month in Upper Gooseberry, Vermont, Baz Rathbone's faux-cremation/skull-trade operation was pretty much back to its usual brisk business. He had made it out of Rankin, New York, in the nick of time. In light of PWADS sudden departure, Sylvester Quinn of the town's BBB had done some poking around and what he'd found had convinced him that Baz had not been on the up and up. Quinn had spread the word to other Better Business Bureaus throughout New England to be on the lookout for PWADS and its owner, Mr. Baz Rathbone. Assuming that something like this might have occurred, Baz – now known as Bart Zuber – had reopened in Upper Gooseberry in the guise of Zuber's Affordable Cremations.

The new office was now furnished with plush chairs and a settee – "living well is the best revenge" was one of Baz/Bart's favorite sayings – and he had made the cabin on Roaring Goose Creek at least reasonably habitable. In the past two weeks, he had attracted his first Vermont customers. New widows Ada Jones and Rita Underwood, as well as Bob Hatfield, a recent widower, had all sought out Mr. Zuber's services and each had been sent an urn containing ashes purported to be the cremains of her or his late spouse. Baz/Bart (henceforth for a while, just Bart) had even picked up a second-hand backhoe and was busily using it alongside Roaring Goose Creek. And, best of all, he had attracted several new customers for human skulls; Captain Kidd was not among them, but that was OK with Bart since the Captain had smelled like trouble from the very start.

As April was coming to an end, Bart was sufficiently confident about still being two steps ahead of the law to make a call to his contact at the Southlands Zoo requesting information about the dead ape that institution was holding. He learned from R. C. McNutt (who was named for the cola that tastes so good with a MoonPie) that the body of Clyde the orangutan was scheduled to leave the zoo on May 8th. Uli Helmsman, a taxidermist now living in Maine who had previously worked at Southlands, would be the one picking up the carcass. R. C. had seen a headshot photograph of Uli and was confident that he could recognize him. After that, provided he got a good look at Helmsman's "vee-hick-al," R. C. figured he'd have no trouble trailing the taxidermist out of town and swiping the ape in the dead of night. Once he had the orangutan in his possession, R. C. would call Bart (who he still knew as Baz) and they would arrange a drop-off at Bart's convenience. Did Bart want to move forward with this plan? "Absolutely," was the answer and so the plot was set in motion.

~ ~ ~

As May 1st approached, preparations for Lazlo and Uli's southern trip picked up speed. Ron arranged his schedule so he would be at the Moose Wallow branch of Styx's Mortuary for the period of Lazlo's absence. He also made the final phone calls to the family of Mrs. Josie May Sagler on Hilton Head. Lazlo was given a contact number for the Saglers and also directions to their condo. Between the directions and his GPS, Laz figured he'd have no trouble finding the late Josie May's grieving kinfolks.

Lazlo had his van serviced in preparation for long-distance driving and he laid in an assortment of snacks for the road. His boss contributed a new set of tires in light of the fact that the trip was partly to transport a body back to the mortuary. He also gave Lazlo a Styx's Mortuary credit card to use for gas, motels, and meals. Lazlo promised solemnly that he would use the card with discretion.

Uli washed two shirts and four pairs of underwear, and bought a new baseball cap in preparation for the trip. He also fished around in his closet and located his swim trunks just in case they stayed at a motel with a pool. He carefully laid out the amount of marijuana he thought they'd need for the trip (a lot) and added his own favorites to the snack collection: Cheetos, Little Debbie's Cosmic Brownies, and Nutella.

On D-day minus three, Lazlo walked into the mortuary's main office only to be brought to a dead halt by Annette's glaring expression. "Hey, A-Fib," he said. "Why the long face?"

"I'll tell you why the long face, Mr. Road Trip Boy. No one has invited *me* to go on this little jaunt. You and Uli get to have all the fun hauling dead bodies up and down the East Coast, but not me. Noooo, I've got to stay here and help Ron mind the store. Now I ask you, is that fair? You'd be grumpy too if you were being left behind."

"Jeez, A-Fib, honey, I'm sorry," said Lazlo. "Of course you can come, if you want to. Three of us can fit in the van, no problem, and there'll still be plenty of room for suitcases and a couple of dead bodies. Have you asked Ron for the time off?"

"Yeah. He said transporting corpses is a routine part of the mortuary business these days and so he had no problem with me tagging along. He said he was unsure how much of a Y-chromosome thing the trip is for you and Uli, however. So, do you two big, strong men want to be alone for a male-bonding experience or can a poor, delicate, double-X-chromosome creature join in?"

"Sure, A-Fib, by all means pack a suitcase and come join us," said Lazlo. "There's a cushy bucket seat in the rear of the van. Whoever rides back there will be traveling in style. Plus, having three people to share the driving will make the trip easier all round. Do you have any weird driving things I should know about? You're not prone to carsickness, are you? Uli tells me we might be winding through some curvy mountain roads in North Carolina."

"Nope," said Annette, "no annoying road habits. And if you and Uli get to talking guy stuff, I'll just pop in my ear buds and listen to an audiobook. As for snacks, apples, carrots, and granola bars will do fine. But then, I'm sure you and Uli already have those on your food list."

"Uh, yeah, absolutely," said Lazlo unconvincingly.

~ ~ ~

On D-day minus one, Uli brought Bookworm Bear over from his workshop. She had turned out even better than he'd

81

hoped and when he emailed a picture to the folks at the All Creatures Great and Small bookstore, they professed themselves thrilled. The bear *was* pretty bulky, but there would only be a day or two when they would have both Bookworm and Mrs. Sagler in the back of the van.

On May 1st, everyone assembled early at Styx's. Ron brought coffees and cinnamon buns from the Country Girl Diner to get the travelers off to a good start. Trying to hold his coffee between his feet as he ate his pastry, Uli immediately filled one of his shoes as they bounced out of the parking lot, but it did nothing to flatten his mood.

They took US-1 around the eastern edge of Maine, connected with I-95 at Houlton, and then headed south. Twelve hours later, they were just south of New York City and ready to stop for the night. At the motel's front desk, there was a moment of embarrassed confusion when Lazlo and A-Fib couldn't decide whether or not to share a room. True, they had been friends with benefits for several weeks now, but they didn't know if Uli was aware of that aspect of their relationship. After considerable hemming, hawing, and foot shuffling, they got separate rooms for that first night. The whole thing was just too stupid to be continued for the entire trip, however, and so the next day Lazlo and A-Fib spilled the beans to Uli and thereafter they were roommates. Uli's only comment was, "Jeez, A-Fib. You could've had *me*, but instead, you settled for Lazlo. I don't know, girl. Just when I was about to decide that you're pretty durn smart, you go and do a dumb thing like that. I just don't know." A-Fib just giggled and gave Uli a kiss on the cheek.

On the second day, they did a steady ten hours on the road. In Robeson County, North Carolina, they saw their first alligator, a bold three-footer sunning near a drainage ditch. Having never traveled through Dixie, A-Fib was fascinated and at her request they stopped at South of the Border, a well-advertised tourist trap just over the South Carolina line. According to the seemingly endless billboards trumpeting the attractions of South of the Border, the park had a new Reptile Lagoon filled with gators, American crocodiles, and snakes. Since it was time for supper anyway, the guys had no problem about getting off the road for a bit.

As it turned out, the Reptile Lagoon was not quite the "must see" attraction that the billboards claimed. The albino Burmese python was kind of cool, but since no one spoke parseltongue, their interest in the phlegmatic serpent dwindled rapidly. One item that did keep their attention, however, or at least Uli's, was an American crocodile, stuffed and posed in an aggressive stance near the pavilion's entrance. The animal – whose nickname was "Big Mac" in commemoration of its place of capture, Mackenzie, Florida – was huge and would have been the star of the Lagoon except for the fact that sometime in the past its tail had been broken off about halfway down its length. Uli grunted his professional disapproval and went off to find a member of the Lagoon staff.

After just a few minutes, he returned and announced that he'd made arrangements for them to take the crocodile back to Maine so he could repair its damaged appendage.

"Do you think we've got enough room in the van for that critter?" said Lazlo. "A-Fib, you've spent a good deal of time in the back. What do you think?"

"It'll be tight until we unload Bookworm Bear," said Annette, "but, yeah, we can do it."

"OK, Uli," said Lazlo, shaking his head. "Let's get some help and get the dang thing loaded. But this is your one and only souvenir for the trip, understood?"

"Understood," said Uli with a grin.

Thanks to the fact that its tail was broken off, Big Mac was fairly easily nestled into the van between Bookworm Bear and the luggage. Happily, its initial taxidermy job had been well done and so it had little if any odor. The toothy snout was a bit of an obstacle, however, and A-Fib scraped her shin on the croc's teeth almost immediately. Uli joked that it could have been worse. "Look at poor old Captain Hook," he said. "He'd have been happy to escape with just a scraped shin." A-Fib was not impressed by Uli's logic, however, and suggested rather forcefully that they should swap seats.

From South of the Border, it was not quite an hour

before they got to Florence, South Carolina, and their motel for the night. After supper, they sat under a grove of palm trees at the far end of the Ramada Inn's lawn and shared a joint. The next day would get them to Hilton Head Island.

Around mid-morning on the third day, they took a left turn at Hardeeville and followed US-278 to Hilton Head Island. They crossed the bridges over Mackay Creek and then Skull Creek, and then they were on the island proper. The Saglers lived in a nicely appointed condo not far from the Harbor Town Lighthouse and they were delighted to welcome the trio of guests from Maine.

The travelers' first impression of their hosts was that they were the smallest people they'd ever met. At five-feet-two-inches tall, Marvin Sagler could have been Mickey Rooney's brother. Marvin's wife, Cissy, was even shorter. "We're in Munchkinland," thought Lazlo.

"I can't tell you how much it means to us for you to be taking Mother S. back home to be buried," said Cissy Sagler, as they sat on the deck overlooking Heddy Gutter Creek and sipped Bloody Marys. "She'll rest ever so much easier in Maine than she would've down here. She never did get used to the heat."

"We've got everything ready for you," said Marvin. "Mama's sweet little body has been fully embalmed at a local funeral parlor and all of the papers you'll need for transporting her between states are in this envelope." Here he handed a bulky manila envelope to Uli. "She's dressed in her favorite negligee, as per her instructions, and looks real peaceful. Come take a look."

Marvin and Cissy led Uli, Lazlo, and A-Fib into the spacious living room, where an enormous wooden coffin with ornate brass handles sat atop a bier supplied by the Hilton Head mortician. Inside the coffin, Mrs. Josie May Sagler lay in an attitude of peaceful repose. She was a tiny woman with dyed black hair that had been permed into tight curls and rouged cheeks that gave her a hint of life. She looked like the quintessential adored grandmother except for one thing: the neck of her pink peignoir had been deliberately left untied in order to show the top of her "shadow."

"Mother S. was no prude," said Cissy. "'Lay me out proper in my Dior peignoir,' she said. 'And be sure there's a hint of bosom showing.' That was her last request."

The Saglers and their guests stood admiring the late matriarch for several moments. Then A-Fib voiced what Lazlo and Uli were also thinking: "I don't think she'll fit in the van."

"Not fit?" said Marvin Sagler in a startled voice. "What do you mean, not fit?"

"Well, Mr. Sagler," said Lazlo, "I'm afraid our van has limited cargo space and at the moment it has two other fairly large items in the back. Your mother's coffin is just too big for the space available. We were hoping to take her back to Maine in a flexible transport container provided by Styx's Mortuary."

"Do you mean take Mama home in a *body bag*?" said Marvin, clearly horrified.

"I know it sounds awful, Mr. Sagler," said Lazlo, trying hard to sound comforting, "but it is the standard equipment for moving a corpse over a long distance. You can rest assured that we'll be extremely careful to protect your mother's body from harm as we load and unload her, and also during the trip. We'll treat her as if she were our own mom. How tall was your mother when she died, by the way?"

"She was a tiny little thing," said Marvin, still visibly shaken at the thought of his mother traveling in a body bag. "She was five feet tall in her prime, but by the time she died at ninety-seven, she had lost a good three inches of that. Oh dear, well, if she has to travel in your container, then I guess that's the way it will have to be. I hope the ladies at the Garden Club never hear about it, though."

"If you have already purchased that handsome coffin, Mr. Sagler, just ship it up to Maine via FedEx or UPS," said Lazlo. "If not, I can show you a catalog of the containers Styx's Mortuary has to offer. Either way, we will make sure that your mother goes to her final rest in a beautiful, state-of-the-art coffin."

After more drinks on the deck and then lunch at the

Country Club on the Saglers' tab, Cissy brought Laz, Uli, and A-Fib back to the house. Marvin had decided that he'd rather not be present when his mother was repackaged; a quiet walk around the Club's extensive grounds sounded much more soothing.

Given the small size of Josie May's earthly remains, the coffin-to-bag transfer was accomplished quite easily. After zipping the nonagenarian into a new Styx's Riverside Mortuary travel container, Lazlo followed office protocol and attached a luggage tag to the zipper pull. This was not really necessary, of course, since Mrs. Sagler's body would never be out of their possession, but still, it was what Ron Styx had directed Lazlo to do and he was an obedient ass. mortician. Unfortunately, in the haste of their departure from Moose Wallow, Laz had forgotten to grab a Styx's luggage tag and so now he simply took a tag bearing his own name from one of the suitcases and clipped it onto Mrs. Sagler. Finally, after all of the repackaging was complete, Josie May was tucked into the van beside Bookworm Bear, under the tailless croc (who was bulky, but pretty light), and next to the luggage. She seemed happy enough with the arrangement.

"Thank goodness we're going to unload the bear before we take on Clyde's carcass," said Lazlo to Uli. "I'm starting to think we made a mistake by adding that croc to our load."

"We'll be OK, little buddy," said Uli. "Snug, but OK. And I could hardly have left the croc in such horrible condition, now could I?"

"Uh," grunted Lazlo.

After saying goodbye to Cissy Sagler and thanking her and Marvin – he in absentia – for their hospitality, the three travelers climbed into the van and headed back to I-95. They turned northwest at Pooler, Georgia, and then drove through Statesboro, Millen, Waynesboro, and Hephzibah on their way into Augusta. The All Creatures Great and Small bookstore was located not too far from the famous August National Golf Club.

Unloading Bookworm Bear and getting her set up inside the store took the rest of the day. The ACG&S owners took their sweet time deciding where the bear would look best –

over near the Bibles or in front of the illustrated Noah's ark books? – and after moving the animal for the fourth time, Uli and Lazlo were pretty well worn out. Nobody argued when Uli suggested that they should drive no further than Aiken, South Carolina, to spend the night.

"We can get some good chitlins in Aiken," said Uli.

"And what might those be?" asked A-Fib.

"Those, lovely A-Fib, are deep fried hog intestines, and no one can call themselves a world traveler until they've tried them," said Uli. "I think they're best washed down with Jack Daniels whiskey, but beer or soda works too."

"Hog intestines?" said A-Fib, with a grimace. "Gag me with a spoon! Can't we just go on up to Charlotte?"

"We can do that tomorrow," said Uli. "Come on, humor the southerner. I can't be in this neck of the woods and not have a plate of chitlins. Then tomorrow it's up to Charlotte, pick up Clyde, and then head for home." Little did they know that heading for home was going to be the most dangerous part of their trip.

Chapter Fourteen

It was May 8th, DOPUD – dead orang pick up day. With A-Fib dozing in the back seat and Uli humming Simon and Garfunkel's *At the Zoo* ("...orangutans are skeptical..."), Lazlo navigated his way up I-20 to Columbia and then I-77 to Charlotte. With only tiny Josie May Sagler and the stuffed croc in the back, the van seemed quite spacious. "One more stop and then home," thought Lazlo, "piece of cake."

Evil forces were afoot, however, nearest and most immediately that of R. C. McNutt. R. C. spent all day on May 8th trimming the shrubbery near the Southland Zoo's medical wing, the Jack Hanna Building. This was where injured animals were brought for treatment and the bodies of deceased animals were put in cold storage until they could be incinerated or otherwise disposed of. Clyde the orangutan fell into the latter category, of course. For many years a great favorite of zoo-goers, Clyde was going to be preserved by taxidermy and then put on display in the lobby of the Marlin Perkins primate house. The current notion was to pose Clyde atop a barrel that matched the orange color of his fur. A sign on the barrel would invite visitors to contribute to the upkeep of the primate facility and the care of its residents. Everyone at Southlands agreed that it was a brilliant plan.

It was approaching eleven o'clock when McNutt watched a white van pull into the parking lot of the Hanna Building. The van's Maine plates verified that this was Clyde's pick up, probably driven by Uli (or was it Ugly?) Helmsman. "Maybe this guy will be a shrimp," thought R. C. McNutt to himself. "Then I could just threaten to kick his ass and he'd run off and leave me with the ape." R. C. was due for a multifaceted disappointment, however. Not one, but *three* people – a tall blonde hottie and two men – got out of the van and headed into the medical unit. One of the guys was about R. C.'s size, but the other one, who he recognized from the headshot as Uli Helmsman, was as big as Mount Mitchell! In a one-on-

one with that guy, R. C. knew exactly whose ass would get kicked.

After about thirty minutes the trio emerged accompanied by the zoo's head veterinarian. Since the foursome ambled off toward the zoo's restaurant, R. C. assumed that they were going to lunch. He took advantage of their absence to give the van a thorough inspection, albeit from a distance. There appeared to be nothing special about the vehicle except for an extra hasp-and-staple and a large padlock on the rear doors. To make sure the extra lock was not a problem, R. C. went to the groundskeepers' storage shed and collected a pair of heavy-duty bolt cutters. Then he went back to his vigil.

By one o'clock, lunch had been eaten and the carcass transfer had been completed. The big guy had come out of the Hanna Building carrying an orang-sized body bag over his shoulder. "Shit, he's big," muttered R.C., concluding that the smart thing to do was to bring help that evening, even though that would mean splitting the fee that Baz Rathbone had promised him. Oh well, there was nothing for it but to call in reinforcements. His pal Foley Wilson, although sort of simple minded, was pretty good in a fight. R. C. always preferred to avoid punch-outs, but sometimes there was no other way.

After a round of farewell handshakes, the three Mainers piled into the van and drove away. Jumping into his battered Taurus, R. C. followed them – at a discrete distance – out of the zoo's back entrance and then through the city of Charlotte. It soon became clear that they were headed for I-85, a mainly east-west route that turns sharply north at Durham and then joins up with I-95 in southern Virginia. R. C. pulled out his iPhone and dialed Foley's number. Foley lived right off I-85 up in Concord, North Carolina, and if he was at home, it would be simple enough for him to join the convoy at the Kannapolis exit. As it happened, Foley was not only at home, but he was very interested in joining the fun. He assured R. C. that he'd be driving right behind him in just a few minutes, and in just a few minutes that was indeed the case. "Bring a mask," R. C. had told him.

The three-vehicle convoy had been rolling along for a few hours and had reached Durham when the van surprised R. C. by exiting from the interstate. It turned onto NC-98 and headed due east through Wake Forest and then on toward Rocky Mount. R. C.'s iPhone rang; it was Foley.

"What the hell are they doing, R. C.?" said Foley in a mountain drawl you could have cut with a knife.

"I don't know, bro," said R. C. "I had them figured for a straight shot up I-85 to Petersburg. Maybe they've got an errand to run in Rocky Mount. All we can do is stay on their tail. You OK back there?"

"Oh, hell yes," said Foley. "I grabbed a six-pack before I left the house and so I'm good for miles and miles. I also brought a Mason jar in case I need to piss and can't take the time to stop."

"Damn, Foley. You are about the most countrified person I've ever met. A Mason jar? I'm glad we're not riding together," said R. C. with a laugh.

And as it turned out, R. C.'s guess wasn't that far off the mark. Uli simply couldn't bear to leave North Carolina without one more taste of Piedmont barbeque – slow cooked, pulled pork served up with vinegar-based red sauce and hushpuppies. "You'll think you've died and gone to Heaven," Uli told Lazlo and A-Fib.

As the van cruised into Rocky Mount, Uli gave Lazlo directions to Aunt Jenny's Downhome Café. Since the restaurant was just off I-95, Aunt Jenny also ran a motel at the same location, said Uli, and if everyone agreed, they could bed down in Rocky Mount for the night. The plan made sense to Lazlo and A-Fib, especially since the following day would be a long one on the road.

Dinner at the Downhome Café also made sense to R. C. McNutt and Foley Wilson, who pulled their respective cars into the parking lot only minutes after the van with the Maine plates. The two thieves entered the diner and took a booth near the back wall. R. C. pointed out their soon-to-be victims.

"Umm, R. C.," said Foley, "the bearded guy is a big 'un, ain't he?"

"Yeah, he's good size," said R. C. "That's why I called you. I figured it might take two of us to scare them off. Those boys will want to protect that pretty little lady, after all."

"Do you think it's gonna come to a fight then, R.C.?" asked Foley with a gulp. His voice betrayed the fact that he was having second thoughts.

"Not if I can help it," said R. C. "Here's my plan. I'm guessing that they're done driving for today. After all, Aunt Jenny has a nice motel just across the interstate and barbeque is always best if it's washed down with several beers. So, if I'm right and they do go across the road and check in, we'll wait an hour or so and then move your car twenty miles up the road to Enfield. There's a big strip mall on Route 481 where we can park it and no one will notice. Then we bring my car back and start keeping a sharp watch on the motel parking lot. Got it so far?"

"Yeah, chief," said Foley. "So far, so good. Move my car and come back. Sit in your car and watch their van."

"Good," said R. C. "I figure we wait until about two in the morning, which should give them plenty of time to go to sleep. Then we quietly steal their van and I drive it up to Roanoke Rapids with you following in my car. In Roanoke Rapids, we'll crack the van open and steal the ape. Then I'll drive you back to Enfield, pay you off, and you can head for home. I'll turn around and start the drive north. The van stays where we empty it."

"Sweet," said Foley. "Whereabouts do you drop off the ape?"

"Don't know yet," said R. C. "After I've got it and I'm on the road, I'll call the guy up north who's financing this whole deal. He and I haven't worked out the details of the transfer, but I'm gonna try like hell to make sure I don't have to drive the damn thing all the way to New England. Here comes the waitress. You ready to order?"

As expected at Aunt Jenny's Café, everyone had a delicious supper. The trio from Maine washed their food down with beer (the guys) or soda (A-Fib), while R.C. and Foley each opted for a large dose of Dutch courage in the form of Jack Daniels whisky. Later, when Lazlo, A-Fib, and

Uli fulfilled R. C.'s prediction by moving the van across the highway to Aunt Jenny's Downhome Motel and checking in, they were all relatively sober. In contrast, when R. C. and Foley moved the latter's car to Enfield and then set up their surveillance of the van, they were three sheets to the wind.

~ ~ ~

At 2:00 a.m. sharp, the alarm on R. C.'s watch went off. The van was still right where it had been parked a few hours earlier. Rousing himself and trying, unsuccessfully, to shake the whiskey cobwebs out of his head, R. C. prodded Foley awake.

"Time to do this," said R. C. "Let's get our masks on."

"Affirmative, chief. I ten-four your ten-thirteen," said Foley, who, like R. C., had been in the military police.

"Dammit, Foley, you just told me you 'understand my transmission' about an 'animal incident,'" said R. C. "Drop the military crap, will you?"

"Roger that, boss," said Foley, oblivious of his continuing disobedience.

The actual theft of the van should have been as easy as falling off a log. Lazlo had left the driver's side window slightly cracked in case Clyde ripened up overnight and R. C. had merely to snake in a bent coat hanger and fish for the latch. Unfortunately, the best laid schemes of mice and body snatchers often go awry, and the complicating factor in this case was that when R. C. climbed into the van, he found Annette Fibrowski asleep on the back seat.

Her presence there had a ready explanation, i.e., Lazlo snored like a buzz saw, especially after a heavy meal. After trying unsuccessfully for three hours to go to sleep next to him, A-Fib had abandoned the effort, gotten dressed, and headed, with a pillow and blanket in tow, for the quietude of the van's back seat. "Something has to be done about that boy's snoring or this relationship has no future," she thought ruefully. "Tomorrow I'm buying Lazlo some of those Breathe Right strips." Thanks to the lasting effects of their Jack Daniels, R. C. and Foley had slept straight through A-Fib's return to the van.

"Hey, what the hell are you doing?" yelled A-Fib as she

jerked awake and found a masked man in the vehicle's driver's seat.

"Holy shit! Who's back there? Dammit, girl. Where did you come from?" yelled R. C. as he tried to deep-breathe himself out of a heart attack.

"Never mind where I came from. What are you doing stealing this van? I'm calling 911 right now," said A-Fib, pulling out her iPhone.

"I don't think so, missy," said Foley, who was now leaning in behind McNutt and pointing a semiautomatic pistol toward their unwanted guest. "Gimme that phone and don't make a peep."

A-Fib had little choice but to do as she was told, and in a matter of seconds she found herself gagged, tied up, and belted into the rear seat. She remained silently staring at the masked driver as the van pulled onto I-95 and headed north. The man with the gun, she realized, was right behind them in a second vehicle.

Some forty-five miles up the road, they took the exit for Roanoke Rapids, a town that R. C. knew well. Then they drove to Cedarwood Cemetery, a secluded burying ground near the dam. They parked the car and van on Eternity Circle in the back of the cemetery, and all three of them got out. Foley kept a close eye on A-Fib while McNutt opened the trunk of the car and retrieved a pair of bolt cutters. Then, in anticipation of some heavy work, R. C. stashed his own cell phone on the van's dashboard so he wouldn't lose it.

Although R. C. might have examined the contents of the van simply by turning on the dome light when he first gained entrance, in his still intoxicated state – and especially after A-Fib's unexpected appearance – that had never occurred to him. So the first look he and Foley got of the vehicle's contents came when R. C. opened the now-unlocked rear doors and shone his flashlight directly into the gaping jaws of Big Mac the croc.

"Oh Mama! Holy shit!" screamed Foley, as he jumped back from the van. "Look out, R. C.! I'll kill the bastard!" Before McNutt could stop him, Foley had pulled out his pistol and emptied the clip in the general direction of the stuffed animal. "Die, you bastard! Die!" Foley kept screaming as he fired.

While Foley was killing the already dead crocodile a thousand times over, R. C. had staggered over to his car, slumped against it, and wet himself. "Oh please, Jesus," he moaned, "if that's Satan, please save me! Don't let those teeth get me! I'll be a better person. I promise." He would probably have driven off right then leaving Foley and the girl to work out their own salvation, except for the fact that Foley had the car keys. As he stood there hyperventilating and peeing, R. C. had sufficient time to actually start thinking about their situation. His first thought was how near he had come to being killed by his partner.

"Dammit, Foley, you 'bout shot me!" screamed R. C. "Put that gun away! You're gonna bring the cops down on us, for sure. Can you see what the hell's in the van? All I saw were teeth about six inches long. Here's the light. Go take a look. I'll watch the girl to be sure she don't run off."

Foley did as he was told. "It's a god-awful huge gator, R. C.," he reported.

"Damn you, don't use my name, asshole."

"Sorry, R. C., I didn't know your name *was* Asshole. I'll try and remember. Anyway, it's a stuffed gator and super dead now that I put about a dozen slugs through it. A couple other shots went wild on me. There are also two big bags in there, about the size of a man. Want me to pull them out for inspection?"

"Yeah, you do that," said R. C., now back to normal albeit a bit damper than before.

Foley reached into the van's cargo area and slid first one and then the other body bag out of the vehicle and onto the ground. He unzipped Mrs. Sagler's bag first.

"Uh oh, Asshole," he said. "This one's a human. Tiny and all shriveled up, but a human being if I ever saw one. I thought we were after an ape."

"We *are* after an ape and don't call me asshole, asshole!" said R. C. "Don't call me anything! Little missy here has big ears, get it? Let me see what you've got there."

When R. C. peered into the body bag, he saw that Foley

was right. The face staring up at him was that of an elderly woman. And not only that, but an elderly woman who was the spitting image of his dearly departed grandma, Maud McNutt. A shiver ran down his spine. "What's in the other bag?" he barked at Foley.

"Jeez, I wish you'd make up your mind about the name thing," muttered Foley as he unzipped the second container. "Well, hello, looka here. This second bag actually has an honest-to-goodness ape in it. Lots of hair, long arms, the whole deal. Uh oh – damn it! It's got a bullet hole right between the eyes. Must've been one of my loose slugs. So we've got a human and an ape. You gonna keep both of them or throw one back?"

"For now, I'm going to keep both of them," said R. C. "Which one looks heavier?"

"I'd say the ape," said Foley, after taking a second look at each corpse.

"OK, you load that one in the trunk of my car while I watch the girl. Then we'll swap jobs and I'll load the other."

Foley knew a bad deal when he heard one, but then he was starting to think this whole thing was a bad deal anyhow. He had signed on to help R. C. steal a dead ape, but now he found himself helping to steal a human corpse as well, and being an accomplice in a kidnapping. Nonetheless, having no better plan, Foley did as he was told.

"OK," said R. C. "Take the flashlight and search the van to see if there's anything else of value we can take." Once again, Foley did as he was told.

After a couple of minutes, Foley returned with three items: a cell phone with a bullet hole through the middle, a paper bag filled with road snacks, and a second bag overflowing with marijuana joints. He was looking distinctly guilty.

"Did you find anything?" asked R. C.

"Uh, well," said Foley, "I found your iPhone sitting on the dashboard all shot up. I guess a wild shot took it out. Sorry, R. C. Here's the girl's phone though, so you can still make calls. It's newer than yours, so really you've come out ahead on the deal."

"You colossal fuck-up," snapped R. C. "Gimme that damn phone. What else have you got there?"

"A bag full of snacks and another one with a nice collection of doobies," said Foley. "Care for something in a joint?"

McNutt agreed that all in all he was indeed ready for a joint and the two men made their selections, lit up, and leaned against the car smoking dope.

"All right, here's what happens next," said R. C. a few moments later, now considerably calmer. "I'm gonna pay you off, drive you to your car, and then your part's done. Take side roads back home and you shouldn't run afoul of the law."

"Fine by me," said Foley. "What about you?"

"I'll be heading north with two carcasses and Miss Nosey here. I've got to do some thinking about what to do with her."

Shortly thereafter, money changed hands and R. C.'s car, complete with four people (one deceased) and a dead ape, left the cemetery. The white van was abandoned where it had been parked and Eternity Circle returned to its usual pre-dawn tranquility.

Chapter Fifteen

It had not been the best pledging season that Stonewall State College's chapter of Kappa Lambda Damnda had ever seen. This year's pledges were mostly "geek squad" material, good for keeping the chapter's academic average up and preventing disciplinary action by the Dean of Students, but not the "party hearty" new members the brothers were hoping for. Nonetheless, the pledge trainer had done his best and tonight was initiation night.

In accordance with ancient (i.e., 1955) Damnda tradition, the pledges were sent out in the dead of night to search for brotherhood. Of course, any fool could have figured out that this was a metaphoric search; brotherhood was to be found in the common pursuit of their objective, not in the form of some object that the pledges would find if they looked hard enough. Unfortunately, these pledges were not just *any* fools; they were priceless fools and they were on a mission.

During the police interrogations that followed the incident, no one could remember why they'd decided to go to Cedarwood Cemetery at three in the morning in search of brotherhood. "Maybe because we could search for brotherhood and drink beer at the same time?" suggested one scared kid. In any event, Cedarwood was where the pledges had headed and it wasn't long before they'd spotted the white van parked on Eternity Circle. Elroy Jenkins, president of the pledge class, said he thought they should check it out.

As Elroy and several other students milled around the van, one spotted an insignia that caught his attention. Lazlo had purchased the vehicle on Long Island and the dealership's metal emblem was prominently displayed on the left rear door: TWO BROTHERS AUTO SALES.

"Hey, Elroy, take a peep at this!" shouted the discoverer,

thrilled at what he had found.

"Well, Peanut, you old dog, look at that, would you?" drawled Jenkins. "'TWO BROTHERS AUTO SALES' – man, that's the best thing we've come up with all night. We can break off that AUTO SALES bit without any trouble and what's left? Only pure brotherhood, that's what. Pop that dude off there, why don't you?"

One of the other pledges produced a Swiss Army knife and after a bit of prying, the metal emblem came right off. Pledge President Jenkins put it in his pocket. The pledge trainer would be pleased.

"I reckon we ought to see if there's anything inside this here van, boys," said Jenkins. "Open her up."

When the pledges opened the van's rear doors, they found it was mostly empty. The only thing inside was a stuffed crocodile that sometime in its history had been badly shot-up. Despite the croc's poor condition – its tail was broken off in addition to the bullet holes – the young men decided that they'd haul it back to the frat house. One suggested that they leave it right outside the small apartment occupied by Mrs. Sourby, their cranky housemother. "It'll scare her right out of her drawers!" he said with a laugh. And so, although no one really wanted to see Mrs. Sourby in that condition, they took Big Mac away with them in all his bits and pieces. Only after the SUV carrying the croc had left the premises did Elroy Jenkins have a crisis of conscience and call the Roanoke Rapids police to report the abandoned van.

~ ~ ~

Lazlo awoke to find a note where A-Fib's pillow should have been. It read: "I'm OK, just gone to sleep in van. Too much snoring!" Believing what the note said about A-Fib being all right, Lazlo shaved and showered.

His relaxed morning ritual was rudely interrupted when Uli, who always saved time in the morning by not shaving, came banging on the door. "Hey, Laz! The van's gone!" shouted Uli.

Lazlo ran to the door, pulled it open and said, "What? The van's gone? But that can't be right 'cause A-Fib is *in* the van. You reckon she went for a drive? Nope, here's the only set of keys. Shit! I hope nothing's happened to her."

The two men ran downstairs and out into the parking lot. The only thing they found in the space where the van had been parked was a bent coat hanger.

"Aw crap, man!" said Uli. "That's the sort of tool a car thief uses. I sure hope somebody didn't steal the van with Annette inside."

Just the thought of A-Fib being kidnapped by car thieves scared the bejesus out of Lazlo. He ran back to the motel's main desk panting and shouting, "Police! A-Fib! Police! A-Fib!"

"What's the problem?" asked the manager as he came running to see what the shouting was about. Then hearing what Lazlo was saying, he yelled to the desk clerk, "This man is having a medical emergency. He has atrial fibrillation and must be having a severe attack. Call 911 immediately!" The desk clerk raced to the nearest phone and made the call just as Lazlo gave way to a full cataplectic collapse.

Ten minutes later, Lazlo was on his way to the ER. He was without both A-Fib and Uli since the EMTs had prevented the latter from riding in the ambulance, saying he was not next of kin. Uli did his best to tell them that Lazlo suffered from narcolepsy and that that was what had caused him to topple over, not an attack of atrial fibrillation. The Med Techs had their hands full, however, and paid no attention to whatever it was the bearded guy was saying.

When the Rocky Mount cops also responded to the 911 call, Uli reported both the theft of Lazlo's van and the disappearance of Ms. Annette Fibrowski, who he had reason to think was inside the van when it was taken. Ms. Fibrowski, said Uli, was Mr. Wetzo's girlfriend and she went by the nickname of A-Fib. *That* was what Mr. Wetzo had been trying to say when he keeled over, that A-Fib was in danger.

"And what's your name, sir?" said Sergeant Willy Pelton, the officer in charge. "What's your connection to Ms. Fibrowski and Mr. Wetzo?"

"My name is Uliba Helmsman, officer" said Uli, "and Annette, Lazlo, and I are all friends from Moose Wallow, Maine. We're traveling together." Then, thinking it might not hurt to give himself a bit of local street cred, Uli slipped in the fact that he was a native North Carolinian and kin to the late senator of the same surname.

When asked, Uli was able to give the police a full description of the stolen vehicle and its cargo. Sergeant Pelton showed no reaction to the van's specs, but his eyes widened when Uli described what it was carrying.

"Well," said Uli, "first and foremost, the van contained the embalmed body of Mrs. Josie May Sagler, who we were transporting from Hilton Head Island back to Maine for burial. Mr. Wetzo – Lazlo – is the assistant mortician at Styx's Riverside Mortuary back in Moose Wallow. I'm sure you'll find all of the paperwork covering Mrs. Sagler's inter- state transport in Lazlo's room. The van also held the body of an adult male orangutan that the Southlands Zoo over in Charlotte had signed over to me to take back to my taxidermy shop in Maine and stuff. I've got those papers in my luggage, if you want to see them. Finally, the van contained the preserved body of a large American crocodile that we picked up at South of the Border on our way down last week. Its tail needs to be reattached and I was taking it back to my shop for the necessary repairs. That's about it," said Uli, neglecting to mention the thirty or so marijuana cigarettes that were stored in the van's glove box. "Maybe we'll luck out and the cops won't find them," he thought to himself.

When the Rocky Mount police ran the specs of Lazlo's van against the list of recently impounded cars in the area, they came up with an immediate match: a vehicle found in the Cedarwood Cemetery in Roanoke Rapids.

"We found your friend's van, Mr. Helmsman," said Sergeant Pelton. "Whoever stole it abandoned it in a graveyard up in Roanoke Rapids. It's in good condition, although there were several bullet holes in the walls and floor of the cargo area. Were those bullet holes present before the theft?"

"Not to my knowledge," said Uli, "but Lazlo's the best one to answer that question. Any sign of Annette?"

"No. That's the bad news," said Pelton. "The good news,

however, is that there's no blood associated with the bullet holes, only what appears to be bits of animal skin of some sort. The lab guys will make a positive identification in a day or two."

"And what about the van's cargo? Any sign of Mrs. Sagler's body or Clyde the ape or the stuffed croc?"

"The vehicle has been cleaned out, I'm afraid, sir," said Pelton. "Even the glove box had been rummaged through and emptied." ("Thank the good Lord for that!" thought Uli.) "Whoever took the van is looking at a long list of serious crimes: kidnapping Ms. Fibrowski, 'displacing' Mrs. Sagler's corpse, stealing both the ape and the crocodile, and auto theft. If we can catch him – assuming the perp is a man – he's looking at a lot of jail time."

"OK, well, listen," said Uli, "let me go tell the desk clerk that we can't check out of our rooms just yet. Then can somebody give me a lift to the hospital? My guess is that Lazlo has come back to life by now and needs rescuing from the medics. After all, there's nothing really wrong with him. He just got excited about A-Fib – I mean his girlfriend – being snatched and he cataplexed out on us."

"Sure, Mr. Helmsman," said the sergeant. "I can give you a lift to the ER. But listen, I gotta ask, are you *really* kin to Senator Les E.? He's a major hero around here. I can't wait to tell my mama that I met his cousin. Would you mind signing the back of this receipt from Dunkin' Donuts? Mama'll treasure it forever."

"Yeah, Sergeant, I really am Senator Les E.'s cousin. We lost a great one when we lost him. Now, how about that ride?"

CHAPTER SIXTEEN

At 4:30 a.m., Annette – her hands and feet still tied and a foul tasting gag stuffed in her mouth – found herself in the front seat of a car traveling north on I-95 with a masked man at the wheel. Her captor had taken her iPhone and she had been roughed up a bit during the hogtying, but otherwise, she was all right. In the trunk, the bodies of Josie May Sagler and Clyde the orangutan occasionally made soft thumping noises as they slid from side to side. Judging from the signs over the highway, A-Fib knew they were approaching Petersburg, Virginia, although at the moment they were still driving through rolling woods and farmland. She decided to try to communicate with her captor.

"Nuhhh!" said A-Fib, looking toward the driver. "NUHHH!"

"What the hell are you trying to say, missy?" said R. C. McNutt. "If I take that gag out, will you keep a civil tongue in your head? Believe me, I'm not much happier about this situation than you are."

A-Fib nodded "yes" to R. C.'s question about keeping a civil tongue in her head and in a rare moment of compassion, he reached over and loosened her gag.

"Yuck! Thanks!" she said. "That thing tastes *awful*! I hope it wasn't used for anything *too* nasty before you stuffed it in my mouth."

"You've got me," said R. C. "I think it was my assistant's pocket handkerchief, but I can't be sure."

"Oh god," groaned A-Fib, "you'd better pull over because I'm gonna puke in about a second."

Not wanting to wear the woman's partially digested supper, R. C. took her suggestion and pulled onto the shoulder of the road. He opened the passenger's side door enough for her to lean out and barf onto the pavement. When she had finished, he pulled her back into the car and gave her a sip of water from a plastic bottle.

"Feel better?" he asked.

"Yeah, a little, I guess," said A-Fib. "What are you going to do with me?"

"I don't know yet," said R. C. honestly. "This was not supposed to be a kidnapping, believe you me. You just happened to be in the wrong place at the wrong time. I'm trying to work out how it ends."

They rode in silence for a few minutes and then A-Fib said, "What smells so bad in here? It's like the smell of a dirty bathroom or a subway tunnel."

"Yeah, well, too bad about that," said R. C. "The fact of the matter is that that stuffed croc scared the piss out of me. Be thankful you're not sitting in it like I am."

More silence. The sun would be coming up in another hour or so.

"Listen, Mr. R. C. Asshole, which is what I think I heard your partner call you. Why don't you just let me go?" asked A-Fib. "I haven't seen your face, so I can't identify you. I won't even press charges."

"My name's *not* Asshole," said R. C. heatedly. "Just R. C."

"OK, Just R. C. What about it? Will you let me go?"

"Shut up, will you? I can't think if you're jabbering away at me. I knew taking that gag out was a bad idea."

"Listen, Just R. C. Maybe I can help you think it through. I minored in psychology and in social work, so I'm pretty good at helping people deal with life crises, which is what I think we are both having."

"Look, it's 'R. C.' Not 'Just R. C.' and certainly not 'Asshole.' And I'm not having a life crisis. Shit, next you'll be telling me to stop so we can both talk to a shrink!"

A-Fib gave a big sigh and looked toward the driver. In the pre-dawn darkness, about all she could see was that he was a man about Lazlo's size, but with a smaller frame. His hair was tousled and his face was hidden behind a black hockey mask. His voice sounded more perplexed than threatening.

"I'm just trying to help, R. C. Talking out problems is

essential to any relationship."

"Jeez, girl!" said R. C., glancing over at her. "We don't *have* a relationship! I nabbed you by mistake when I stole the van to get the ape carcass. Now we're on the lam, you hoping you don't get hurt and me hoping I don't go to prison. Does that sound like a relationship to you?"

"Never judge a relationship by its brevity, R. C. We are currently mutually dependent on one another, two souls driving down the interstate of life, each wishing the other would FOAD. That sounds pretty much like some marriages," said A-Fib.

"Sweet Mother McCready!" said R. C. "Will you please just *shut up*?"

A-Fib was silent for a few minutes, but then returned to the role of analyst. "Were you happy as a child, R. C.? Is this all some sort of weird revenge against a domineering mother? Do you view me as your mother, R. C.?"

"Great God Almighty, shut the crap up! I *do not* view you as my mother, with whom I always had a good relationship, by the way. And if I'd known *your* mother, I'd have advised her to never have children. What a pain in the ass you are. As I once told my sharp-tongued ex-wife, 'Shut up, shut up, shut up!'"

"OK," said A-Fib. "Got it. No parental things to work out. And that was excellent grammar by the way."

"Say *what*?" asked R. C., who had *never, ever* been complimented on his grammar.

"You said 'my mother, with whom I always had a good relationship,' not 'my mother, who I always had a good relationship with.' Nice. No ending the sentence with a preposition for you."

"Missy, I have no earthly idea what you're talking about," said R. C.

Silence. Then Annette noticed that the faintest glimmer of the sunrise was starting to be visible on the horizon. If she was going to act, she needed to do it soon.

"Mr. R. C.," she said, "I've got to pee real bad. If you'll untie me for just a minute and let me out to take a leak, I promise I'll come right back. Otherwise, we're both going to be sitting in urine-soaked clothes and the car is really going to stink. What do you say? I'm too tired and stiff to try to get away and we're way out in the country anyhow. Give me a break, will you? I promise not to do any more psychoanalyzing if you'll just LET ME PEE!"

R. C. knew it was a bad idea, a really bad idea, but he also knew that if he didn't get rid of this kid for just a few minutes he was going to lose it completely. So many words! So many questions! He drove until they were in a dip between two hills and then he pulled onto the shoulder for the second time.

"All right, but don't screw this up," he said. "Here's the drill: I'm going to untie you and open the door. You slip over into the grass and do your business. Then you come straight back and I tie you up again. If you mind your manners, I'll leave your feet untied. If you misbehave, I'll tie both your hands and your feet, and I'll put the gag back in. Got it?"

"I got it, R. C.," said A-Fib. "Thanks. I'm about to burst."

R. C. followed his part of the bargain to the letter and Annette, whose mamma didn't raise no fool, double-crossed him immediately. As soon as she got out of the car and over the bank where R. C. could not see her, she ran like mad for a thicket of woods a quarter mile away. Fear removed the stiffness from her limbs and added to her speed. When she had not returned in three minutes, R. C. got out of the car and looked for her. He could see little in the darkness that still shrouded the landscape, but it made no difference since A-Fib was not there to be seen. "Maybe my name *should* be Asshole," he thought to himself as he gunned the car back onto the interstate.

~ ~ ~

Annette had stepped from the shoulder of the highway onto a dew-slippery bank covered with knee-deep grass. It took all of two steps for her to lose her footing and then slide on her backside down to the plowed field. After a couple of seconds to catch her breath and make sure nothing was broken, she was back on her feet and sprinting toward the trees that were just visible on the far side of the field. "The idiot actually let me go! He let me go!" she exulted (silently, of course) as she ran. And when a little voice in her head pointed out that she was taking unfair advantage of an act of kindness, she told it to shut up and kept running.

From the shelter of the woods, she heard the car pull back onto the interstate and roar away. She watched as its rear lights faded in the distance. It wasn't until full daylight, however, that she felt brave enough to leave the trees and start looking for help.

Happily, help wasn't far away. After crossing another plowed field, Annette hit a gravel road that led over a slight rise and into the yard of a neat farmhouse. A big moose of a dog lay sprawled on the front porch and he gave her a perfunctory volley of barking before trotting over with his tail wagging. On the dog's heels came the farmer and his wife, accompanied by the smells of coffee and bacon.

Dean and Etta Jones listened to Annette's story with headshakes and words of sympathy.

"Never heard such a durned thing in my whole life," said Dean.

"Me neither," agreed Etta, "but you just come this way into the kitchen, honey. We've got to get you cleaned up and fed. I'll bet you're famished."

"I am hungry, that's for sure," said Annette. "Mostly though, I'd like to brush the taste of that gag out of my mouth. You don't happen to have an extra toothbrush, do you?"

"Of course, we do, darling. You just follow me," said Etta as she led the way. "Dean, you go call the sheriff while I'm getting Annette cleaned up a little and then fed some breakfast."

When the Dinwiddie County sheriff arrived, Annette told her story between bites from a huge plate of bacon and eggs. She had been spending the night in Rocky Mount, North Carolina, she said, along with two friends, Lazlo Wetzo and Uliba Helmsman.

"That last's a pretty familiar name over in North Carolina," noted the Sheriff in passing.

"Senator Helmsman was a cousin of my friend, Uliba," said A-Fib. The Sheriff appeared to listen more closely than before.

"Anyway," continued Annette, "for personal reasons, I left my motel room and went out to sleep in our van, but I hadn't been there long when two guys broke in. One of them seemed to be the boss and the other one his helper. When they found me in the back seat, they grabbed me and tied me up. Then we all drove a few miles to some cemetery – the boss and me in the van and the helper following in a car. At the cemetery, they looted the van. There was some gunfire at the cemetery, but only because one of the things in the van scared the thieves."

"What exactly were you transporting, Ms. Fibrowski?" asked the Sheriff.

"OK, this is going to sound weird, but bear with me. My friend Lazlo is a mortician and one of the primary reasons we came down from Maine was for him to pick up an embalmed body in Hilton Head and take it back up north for burial."

"The thieves took the body?" asked the Sheriff.

"Yeah," said A-Fib, "and they also took the carcass of an adult male orangutan that we had picked up at the Southlands Zoo in Charlotte. Uli Helmsman is a taxidermist and the zoo has hired him to stuff the ape for display in their primate house."

"One dead human, one dead ape. Did they take anything else?" asked the Sheriff, clearly ready for virtually *any* weirdness at this point.

"I don't think so," said A-Fib, ignoring the stash of joints that she knew R. C. and Foley had lifted from the van's glove box. "There was also a stuffed crocodile in the back that Uli was taking back to Maine to repair before returning it to that South of the Border place in South Carolina, but I think the thieves left that. It must have been the crocodile that scared them when they first opened the back of the van. The helper was so freaked out that he pulled out a pistol and shot the croc full of holes."

"Rapid fire gunshots?" asked the Sheriff.

"Yeah," said A-Fib.

"So, after they took the corpse and the carcass, then what happened?"

"All three of us got into the car and we drove off, leaving the van at the cemetery. We hadn't gone too far before we stopped and let the helper out. I think the boss paid him off at that point. Then the boss and I started driving north."

"Wow," said the Sheriff, "these old boys have done a pretty good night's work as far as the list of charges against them goes. I've got kidnapping, displacing a human corpse, auto theft, stealing that ape carcass, and probably illegal possession of a semiautomatic weapon. I don't suppose you got any names, did you? Or maybe a make and model of the car?"

"Not full names, I'm afraid," said A-Fib. "The boss, the one I tricked into letting me out of his car to go to the bathroom, was called 'R. C.,' or sometimes 'Just R. C.,' or 'R. C. Asshole.' The other one was called 'Foley.' And about all I can tell you about the boss's car is that it's a beat-up four-door sedan of some sort. I hope some of that helps."

"Everything helps, mam," said the Sheriff. "We'll get these guys, don't you worry. The main thing right now is that you're safe. That was quick thinking about needing to empty your bladder. I can't believe the guy went for it."

"Yeah, that's kind of funny. I think R. C. whoever-he-is must have kids. At least, he's got a soft spot of some sort. He told me a couple of times that kidnapping me was not part of the plan. I think he really felt bad for me when I said I needed to pee. Will the law be any easier on him because the kidnapping wasn't planned?"

"I doubt it," said the Sheriff. "But now let's put in a call to the Rocky Mount police and your friends. I'm sure they'll be relieved to hear that you're OK."

The Sheriff phoned Rocky Mount and after all of the official information had been shared, Lazlo was put on the line.

"A-Fib? Is that you? Are you all right, honey?" he said in a panicked voice.

"Hi, Laz. Yeah, I'm fine. I got kidnapped when the van was stolen, but now I'm up in Virginia having breakfast with the local Sheriff and some nice folks named Jones. The kidnappers didn't hurt me or anything, baby, so don't worry yourself about that. But they made off with Mrs. Sagler and Clyde, I'm afraid. Tell Uli I'm sorry."

"He's right here and he says for you not to bother yourself about Clyde," said Lazlo, whose voice was returning to normal along with his breathing. "God, A-Fib, I was so scared. I ran around like a headless chicken, hyperventilated, cataplexed out, and woke up in the ER. But now you're safe! Oh jeez, A-Fib, I love you so much, do you know that?"

"Be careful, Lazlo," said Annette with a chuckle. "Words have consequences. We'll talk all about love and other things when I see you, which I hope will be soon. Yep, the Sheriff is nodding his head 'yes,' which I guess means they're going to drive me back down to Rocky Mount. In the meantime, you and Uli take care, OK?"

"We will, honey. We will. Just get yourself down here," said Lazlo.

CHAPTER SEVENTEEN

After letting Annette slip through his fingers, R. C. McNutt drove north on I-95, cursing himself every mile of the way. What a shithead he was! Somehow he had let a simple car-theft-and-robbery turn into kidnapping, corpse stealing, and God knows what else. If he wasn't careful, he could end up spending the rest of his life in prison and the thought was none too appealing.

"Think, R. C., think!" he kept repeating to himself. "What needs to be done to keep your skinny ass out of jail?"

First and foremost, R. C. decided, he needed to change cars since it was entirely possible that that damned girl had gotten enough of a look at his vehicle to give the cops a good make-and-model. With a car swap in mind, he left the interstate just south of Richmond and drove to the small town of Powhatan, where, conveniently enough, his cousin Raleigh McNutt lived. "I can count on Raleigh for help," said R. C. to himself, forgetting for a moment what a stupid thing that was for a North Carolinian to say.

In the event, Raleigh McNutt was only too pleased to swap his 2006 Smart car for R. C.'s sedan. He had guests arriving in a few days, Raleigh allowed, and it would be nice to be able to drive four people around in comfort. How long did R. C. think he'd need the Smart car? A week? Not a problem. Did R. C. want to explain what was going on? No? Not a problem. Did R. C. have the fifty-dollar car swap fee? Yes? Then Raleigh was as happy as a Chesapeake Bay clam.

The cargo space of the Smart car was just barely adequate for Mrs. Josie May Sagler and Clyde the orangutan. Indeed, Mrs. Sagler needed to be folded up a bit in order to make the packing job a success. Raleigh McNutt watched his cousin wedge the two mystery parcels into the tiny trunk, but true to his word, he asked no questions. Twenty minutes after pulling into Raleigh's driveway, R. C. was driving out.

~ ~ ~

Assuming the search for the missing girl would be most intense along the I-95 corridor, R. C. turned west out of his cousin's driveway and made for the Shenandoah Valley and Interstate 81. As he drove along the winding secondary roads, he wrestled with the fact that he was stealing not only an ape carcass, but also the corpse of a woman who looked exactly like his grandmother. Somehow that second part just didn't seem right. If Heaven was a reality and by some miracle he met Grandma McNutt there some day, she'd have plenty to say about the time he hauled her doppelganger around Virginia in a Smart car. He thought he'd stop somewhere and take another look at the corpse. Maybe he'd been mistaken about the resemblance.

Just west of US-29, R. C. turned off of the highway and onto a fire road that ran into the George Washington National Forest. He continued for about a quarter mile up the dirt track and then stopped and killed the motor. Opening the trunk of the Smart car, he reached in, lifted out the bag he knew held human remains, and unzipped it. A long look inside confirmed his worst fears; the dead woman might have been his grandmother's long-lost twin. Looking at her, he could remember all of those kisses on the forehead, all of those comments about R. C. being her special boy, and all of those Sunday dinners at Granny McNutt's house. And now he was stealing her body.

R. C. replaced the body reverently in the Smart car's trunk. He needed to think and think carefully, but he was in no shape to do so. What he wanted was something to calm his nerves, but what? Then he remembered the marijuana cigarettes in his pocket – just the ticket for a stressed out body snatcher.

Now, unbeknownst to R. C., Lazlo and Uli had included a few "fry sticks" among the joints they'd packed for the trip, that is, joints that had been dipped in embalming fluid and then dried. Although both Laz and Uli knew that fry sticks – also known as sherms, wacks, or wetdaddies – are potentially carcinogenic, their hallucinogenic highs were just too good to bypass entirely. And now R. C. McNutt was about to experience his first "fry stick boogie."

The buzz from the enhanced joint came on gently and pleasantly enough, as did the next stage, that of being really and truly high. Now R. C. was no longer stricken with guilt at the thought of having his dead grandmother in the trunk of his car; rather, he found it unbelievably funny. He laughed until tears ran down his face and he thought his sides would split. Looking down at his joint, he noticed that it seemed to be burning much more slowly than regular doobies, an effect that delighted him to no end.

It was the "stoned" stage that was R. C.'s downfall. Regular fry stick users always warn novices that full intoxication can bring on vivid hallucinations – some pleasant and some distinctly unpleasant; R. C. McNutt's vision was the latter sort of experience. Legions of gray, wrinkled, and obviously dead grannies circled him, pinched him, and jabbed him with sharp sticks, all the time shrieking, "You're *evil*, R. C., *evil*! Let the evil out, boy!" Worse yet, a couple of them stripped off their old lady clothes and tried to seduce him. With saggy breasts swaying and hips shaking, they chanted, "Bury us or marry us, R. C.! Put us in the grave or forever be our slave!" R. C. McNutt flailed wildly at them with his arms and tried to run away, but all to no avail. Mercifully, in his wacked-out efforts to escape his tormentors, he staggered and fell, hitting his head on a rock. He lay there twitching, as if the granny demons were still at work inside his unconscious skull.

~ ~ ~

When he regained consciousness an hour later, R. C. knew – even through his massive headache – what he had to do. He had to get rid of Mrs. Sagler's body, not in a disrespectful way, mind you, but in a way that would get her the hell out of his life forever. And he knew how.

Although it hadn't registered very clearly a few hours before, he now remembered that Mrs. Sagler's body bag had a luggage tag affixed to it. Despite the danger of releasing a new wave of granny demons, R. C. reopened the car's trunk and took a look at that tag. It read:

Lazlo Y. Wetzo
128 Muskrat Love Lane, Apt. 2
Moose Wallow, Maine 04781

R. C. removed the tag and put it in his pocket. Then he repacked the trunk, got back in the car, and drove purposefully into Staunton, Virginia. In Staunton, he stopped at a U-Haul store, where he bought their largest shipping box, a large parcel of bubble wrap, and a roll of strapping tape. Next, after finding a secluded spot at the very back of a truck stop's giant parking lot where he was sure he was alone, R. C. transferred Josie May Sagler from her bag to the shipping box and packed her snuggly with bubble wrap. Several neatly applied strips of packing tape later, and he was ready to take his parcel to the UPS office in a nearby mall. He noted on the shipping form that the box contained "books, teddy bears, and childhood memorabilia," and he was assured by the counter clerk that the parcel would be delivered to the Moose Wallow, Maine, address within three days. R. C. paid for the shipment with a VISA card that he'd found in his cousin Raleigh's car console and that carried the name Ivan Jackson. There were also several other such cards in the console, each with a different name. "Well, well, Cousin Raleigh, you old rascal," chuckled R. C. "Who'd have thunk it?"

It was with a much lighter heart that R. C. pulled onto I-81 to continue his journey north. First, he had gotten shed of that nosy girl who thought she was a psychoanalyst and now he had gotten shed of the old bag that looked like his granny. Now the only cargo he had was the ape carcass – his original objective, after all. That evening he would call Baz Rathbone and make the necessary arrangements for passing the baton named Clyde.

~ ~ ~

The Kappa Lambda Damnda pledge trainer was not amused. Not only had this year's pledge class completely missed the meaning of the "search for brotherhood" assignment, but they had also brought the Roanoke Rapids police home with them. And, perhaps even worse than having to defend the pledges' juvenile actions to the cops – "They're just *college kids*, officer" (an indefensible and disingenuous argument, if there ever was one) – the pledge trainer had the challenge of placating Mrs. Sourby, the KLDs' irascible housemother. Mrs. Sourby had *not* been amused that morning when she stepped out of her apartment and into the gaping jaws of Big Mac. She had cut her toe, ruined a perfectly good set of tights, and gone public with her belief that all the KLDs – pledges and brothers alike – were "fucking shitbirds!" It was going to take more than flowers and candy to get back into Mrs. Sourby's good graces.

For their part, the police – despite the fact that they shared, almost to a man, Mrs. Sourby's take on college students – made life easy for the Kappa Lambda Damndas. They took possession of the stuffed croc, warned the fraternity's officers that this sort of thing must never happen again, and slapped the chapter with a month's suspension of all parties. ("Yeah, right, like that's going to happen," thought the brothers in unison.) After fruitlessly questioning Pledge President Elroy Jenkins to see if he could shed any light on the van thieves' car, the cops took possession of the crocodile and left campus.

And so, by sunset on the same day that the van was stolen and looted, A-Fib was back safe in Lazlo's loving arms, Big Mac the croc had been returned to Uli Helmsman's hairy arms, the van had been returned (a bit shot up, but functional), and Josie May Sagler was on her way to Lazlo's apartment in a UPS truck. The Mainers prepared to resume their journey north.

~ ~ ~

That very same evening, R. C. McNutt placed a call on A-Fib's iPhone to Baz Rathbone at the only number he knew. After eight rings, R. C. was about to hang up when a voice on the other end said, "Zuber here."

"Oh, sorry," said R. C. "I was trying to reach Mr. Baz Rathbone. I thought this was his number. I guess I dialed wrong."

"Who is this?" asked the voice at the other end. "I know Rathbone and can get a message to him."

"Oh yeah?" said R. C. "Well, will you please tell him that R. C. McNutt says 'Clyde is on the way'? He'll know what that means."

As he talked, R. C. was aware of a strange whistling noise on the line. It reminded him of a radiator letting off steam. *Weef! Weef! Weef!* Maybe they had a bad connection.

"McNutt? That you? This is Rathbone speaking. I also go by the name of Zuber at times. Have you got the goods?"

"Yeah, I've got them all right, or 'him' to be more precise. Hey, do you hear a whistling noise on the line?"

"This phone has been whistling like that for a couple of weeks," said Rathbone. "I think the connections got wet when we had the spring thaw. Don't worry about it. Where are you?"

Weef!

"I'm in northeastern Pennsylvania staying in a rat's ass of a motel near Scranton. How do you want to handle the transfer? I'd love to wrap this up and go home."

"OK, I don't think we're too far apart," said Baz. "Hang on while I take a quick look at the Internet."

By the time he returned to the phone, Baz had the rendezvous plan worked out. "Listen, McNutt," he said, "if we each drive about 175 miles, we'll meet up. Here's the deal. When we get off the phone, take a look at a map and find Cowsick Falls, New York. It's on Route 22 and almost due west of Bennington, Vermont. If you drive north on twenty-two past Cowsick, you'll start seeing signs for the Green Mountain Nudist Resort. That's where we'll meet."

Weef!

"You want to make the swap at a nudist camp? Are you nuts?" said R. C.

"Not nuts, just cautious," replied Baz. "Listen, I know this campground. It's heavily wooded and the campsites are far apart. I'll get there before you and set up a tent, and I'll tell the gatekeeper that I'm expecting a guest. All you have to do is show up, get directions to my campsite, drive around there and exchange the ape for cash. You'll only have to strip off long enough to drive from the entrance to my tent and back. Of course, if you want to stay longer, you're welcome to do so. It's a nice place with a beautiful swimming pool and some gorgeous female swimmers."

Weeeef!

"What about the cops?" asked R. C.

"That's the beauty of meeting at a nudist camp," said Baz. "There won't *be* any cops. We couldn't ask for a more private setting. You up for this?"

R. C. thought that that was an unfortunate choice of words given the topic under discussion, but he decided to let it pass. "Well, shit, I guess so," he finally said. "As long as we can do our business and then I can leave. I guess there ain't no harm, especially if you think the setting will throw the cops off the scent."

Weef!

"What do you mean, 'throw the cops off the scent,' McNutt? Do you have any reason to think they know enough to be following you?" asked Baz, suddenly concerned that things might not be going as smoothly as he'd thought.

"Yeah, well, there were some complications back in North Carolina," admitted R. C. "When a pal of mine and I swiped the van that contained the ape, we also got a human corpse and a college girl who was sleeping in the vehicle."

Weef! Weef! Weef!

"Great God Almighty, McNutt!" shouted Baz. "You assured me that this would be a piece of cake. Now it sounds like a simple robbery has turned into kidnapping and God knows what else! Where's the girl?"

"She got away back in Virginia. Ran off into the woods when I let her out of the car in the middle of the night to take a leak. But don't worry. I had a hockey mask on the whole time and so she don't know what I look like, and I've changed cars so the cops don't know what to be on the lookout for. I'm calling you on her iPhone."

Weef!

"What a screw-up you are, McNutt. Does the girl know your name?" asked Baz, who was now pacing back and forth in his office and chain-smoking.

"Only my initials," said R. C. "She thinks my full name is R. C. Asshole."

"Yeah, well, she's certainly dead right about that, isn't she?" said Baz, a tad mean-spiritedly.

Weef!

"And what was that you said about stealing a human body at the same time you got the ape? Do you still have it?" asked Baz, who had begun to recalculate the profit margin on this little venture.

"Nah," said McNutt. "It was the body of an old woman who looked just like my grandmother. The damned thing was freaking me out and so I packaged it up and UPS'd it out of Staunton to an address in Maine. Pretty smart, huh?"

Weef!

"Shitfire, McNutt, you've sure got this whole thing royally screwed up," said an exasperated Baz. "I don't suppose you wore your hockey mask into the UPS store, did you? And I don't suppose you remembered to wipe down the package you mailed in order to remove all of your fingerprints, did you?"

"Well, uh, I was all flustered, you know?" said R. C. defensively. "But I don't think we need to worry about the UPS guy. He didn't seem to be the sharpest tack in the box, if you know what I mean."

"For both our sakes," said Baz, "I hope the old saying that 'it takes one to know one' is true."

Weef!

"Yeah, right," agreed R. C., vaguely suspicious that he'd just been insulted, but not quite sure.

"What are you driving?" asked Baz.

"A blue Smart car," said R. C. "Which means that I'm sitting about a foot away from this ape carcass that you want so bad and the damned thing is starting to smell something fierce."

Weef!

"Damn that bloody whistling!" shouted Baz to no one in particular. "I can't *stand* that noise much longer! Now listen, McNutt, let me get this straight. Adding to the Keystone Cops aspect of this deal, you're driving around in a child-sized car with a rotting ape. That right? You don't by any chance have a circus clown in there with you, do you?"

"Now you're just getting pissy," said R. C. "The Smart car gets good mileage and it hugs the road real nice. Besides, it was the only car my cousin Raleigh could give me as a loaner. And I ain't been nowhere near a town named Keystone."

Weef!

ZZZZIT! SISSSS! WHIRRR! CLICK! GRRREEEKKK! ZZZZIT! POP! ZAP!

Sneerrk!

"What the hell was all that noise?" said Baz. "Did you just wreck your car or something?"

"Naw, man, I'm good," said R. C., "and I sure don't know what that was. It sounded like somebody getting electrocuted or something."

"Come to think of it," said Baz, "an electronic gadget shorting out is *exactly* what it sounded like. I wonder if someone had this line bugged. Repeat the Pledge of Allegiance for me very slowly."

"What the crap are you playing at now?" sputtered R.C.

"Just do it! I want to see if I think the line is clearer now than before."

"'I pledge allegiance to the flag of the United States,' something, something, something," said R. C.

"Yep, I was afraid of that," said Baz, the worry palpable in his voice. "The line is stronger and clearer, and unless I miss my guess, that annoying whistle is gone. I'm afraid some third party heard everything we just said, my friend."

"Damnation, Baz," squeaked R. C., "what are we going to do?"

"Well, for one thing, we're going to ditch the nudist camp plan. Pull over on the shoulder and take a look at 'Settings" on the girl's iPhone," directed Baz. "We need the cell's number as a safe way to communicate."

A minute or so later, R. C. had found the iPhone's number. He read it off to Baz.

"OK," said Baz. "I'm going out to find a public phone so I can call you safely. It may take five or ten minutes. You just sit tight and keep that cell phone turned on. Got it?"

"I got it Baz," said R. C., now miserably aware that he

might end up doing some jail time for this caper. "There's a rest area about a mile down the road. I'll drive on down there and park and wait for you to call."

As it turned out, Baz needed almost thirty minutes to locate what he considered to be a safe public phone. R. C. picked up immediately when the iPhone rang. "Hello. That you, Baz?" he asked.

"You dumb shit," shouted Baz, "stop using our names. The call could have been from one of the girl's friends and now that person would know that a stranger hoping to talk to 'Baz' has her pal's cell phone. Damn! Are you dumb or what?"

"OK, OK! Point taken," said R. C. "What are the new plans?"

"Now listen closely," said Baz, lowering his voice to a hushed tone. "I want you to drive straight to a little town called Williamstown, Massachusetts. Just south of town on Route 7 there's a big Salvation Army store with lots of those drop-off containers out back. People drive by and leave plastic bags full of clothes and stuff at all hours of the day and night. I want you to arrive there at exactly 2:00 a.m. tomorrow morning and leave the bag containing the ape carcass leaning up against the container that's farthest back. Then you drive to the edge of the parking lot, kill your motor and lights, and wait for me. I'll come by about a minute behind you, collect the ape, pull over to your car and pay you off, and the deed is done. You got all that?"

"I guess so," grumbled R. C. "I find this Williamstown place, drop off the ape behind the Salvation Army store, wait for you, get paid, go home. That right? I like that last part best."

"Yeah, me too, pal," said Baz. "I just hope this phone line is clean and that the cops – assuming that was who had my other line bugged – will go off on a wild goose chase to the nudist camp. All right, I'll see you tonight. Don't forget, make your drop at 2:00 a.m. on the dot."

"See you at 2:01," said R. C. "Don't forget my money. See you tonight."

CHAPTER EIGHTEEN

The instant that Tom Mot spilled the contents of his official FBI coffee mug onto his laptop computer, all hell broke loose. Sparks flew, alarms rang, and rainbow colors filled the screen as the laptop ground its way toward electronic death. A thin wisp of smoke curled up from the short-circuited machine. It was a goner and so was Mot's tap on Baz Rathbone's landline.

Mot's yelps and curses brought Steve Nevets running through the door that connected their motel rooms. What he saw was not reassuring. His partner had blood streaming from his nose and he was hopping around like a mad man. Mot was grabbing at the front of his trousers as he hopped, giving one the impression that a bee might somehow have gotten down his pants. "What the hell's up, Tom?" yelled Nevets.

(*Sneerrk!*) "I spilled hot coffee on my computer and fried it!" yelled Mot. (*Sneerrk!*) "And some of the coffee went in my lap and I'm afraid I've fried old Jumbo too!" (*Sneerrk!*) "Shit! THAT HURTS!" (Regarding the reference to "Old Jumbo," LBJ was one of Mot's personal heroes. Enough said.)

"Jeez, Tom! Damn, that's gotta sting like crazy!" said Nevets. "Do you know you've got blood streaming out of your nose as well? I think you might need a doctor or at least some Lidocaine for the burns. Want me to run to the drugstore and get you some?"

After a few minutes of private self-examination of his privates, Mot concluded that applying Lidocaine would be sufficient and so Nevets drove to CVS for the anesthetic cream. Once applied, it quickly brought blessed relief to the burned body parts. In response to Nevets's inquiry about how he was feeling, Mot replied that he was, "Numb in some places and sticky in others. I can't hear very well and I'm really pissed off."

(*Sneerrk!*) "Until I screwed it up, the system was working perfectly, Steve," said Mot, shaking his head in disbelief that he'd botched the tap. (*Sneerrk!*) "Rathbone and his accomplice were spilling their guts about how they pulled off the job and what they planned to do next. Damn it!"

"Tell me more about the tap in a minute, partner," said Nevets. "First, I want to make sure you're OK. You say you can't hear very well. Do you have any idea why?"

"Duh! Because I had my headphones on when the computer blew up, didn't I," said Mot, sarcastically. (*Sneerrk!*) "It was like being in a tunnel when a bomb goes off. About all I can hear now is the ringing in my ears." (*Sneerrk!*)

"Well, one small – very small – benefit may be that your nose has stopped whistling," said Nevets. "You're making 'snerking' sounds because the bleeding has you all stopped up, but the whistling noise is gone. Maybe you blew out an adhesion or something and cleared your nostrils."

(*Sneerrk!*) "Yeah, well, that would be nice," said Mot. "But anyway, let me tell you the rest of what I learned from the tap. Rathbone and a guy named R. C. McNutt, aka R. C. Asshole, were comparing notes about how the dead ape had been snatched and how McNutt should go about delivering the body. Believe it or not, they're going to use a nudist camp near the Vermont and New York state line for the hand-off." (*Sneerrk!*) "Rathbone's going to set up camp there tomorrow and McNutt is going to come for a visit and drop off the ape. Not only do we know when and where the goods will change hands, but we've got one of the perps driving a car a school kid could recognize." (*Sneerrk!*)

"How's that?" asked Nevets.

"McNutt borrowed a blue Smart car from one of his cousins down south! How many Smart cars do you see on the roads of rural New England? Not many, I'm thinking. Anyway, I'm listening to all this stuff and writing it down, thinking to myself, 'we've got you idiots now,' when over goes the coffee mug, zap goes the computer, and poof goes the tap. Damn it! I'll bet those guys are on full alert now. I might as well have cut into their conversation and said, "We're onto to you two creeps." (Sniff!)

"Don't beat yourself up, Tom," counseled Nevets. "You got a lot of good stuff before you drowned your machine. Could you tell from the conversation where these guys are physically located? Oh, and by the way, your 'snerking' has now changed to just sniffing."

"Snerk, sniff, tomayto, tomahto," said Mot. "Anyway, the answer to your question is that McNutt is in Scranton, Pennsylvania, and Rathbone is probably three-to-four-hundred miles away, although I can't be sure in which direction. He said the nudist camp is halfway between their starting points. But listen, Steve, how the hell are we going to nab them in a nudist camp? I'm not up for a bare-ass stake out, especially not with these burns." (*Sniff!*)

"Maybe we can get a husband and wife team from the Albany field office to go to the camp," suggested Nevets. "Give me all the info you've got on McNutt and Rathbone, and I'll put in a call to our people in Albany. This request should make them laugh themselves silly."

It only took a few minutes on the phone for the arrangements to be made. Agents Tina and Larry Armstrong would head for the Green Mountain campground immediately. They would be primarily on the lookout for R. C. McNutt's blue Smart car, and secondarily for a singleton male driving a vehicle with New England plates. The Albany office had offered to send a photographer along to capture the arrest on video, but the Armstrongs had been adamant in saying "no." As soon as there was something to report, the folks in Albany promised to be back on the line to their Boston-based counterparts.

"The thing that worries me," said Mot, "is that the nudist camp scheme was discussed before the tap went up in flames. What if Rathbone and McNutt figured out from all the noise that they'd been bugged? My guess is that they're at least smart enough to change the drop-off plan." (*Sniff!*)

"Well, you could be right, Tom," agreed Nevets. "Too bad there's no way we can track one or both of them as they move around."

"Wait a minute!" shouted Mot. "That's it! McNutt has Annette Fibrowski's iPhone and if it's turned on, we ought to be able to track it using the built-in 'Find My iPhone' app. All we need to do is get Fibrowski's iCloud user name and password. We'll need to hurry though, because once that phone's battery runs out, all of its functions will go dead." (*Sniffle*)

"Tom, sometimes you're a genius," said Nevets, giving his partner a clap on the back. "I'll call Lazlo Wetzo right now. If I can get through to him, Annette Fibrowski shouldn't be far off."

One phone call later and Nevets had the needed information. Using *his* laptop – which he silently vowed Mot would never lay a finger on – Nevets plugged in A-Fib's ID information and cell number. As if by magic, a map appeared on the computer screen indicating that her iPhone was currently in Carbondale, Pennsylvania, a small town about twenty miles northeast of Scranton. The two agents looked at each other. R. C. McNutt was on the move, driving toward his rendezvous with Baz Rathbone. Now, if only that iPhone battery held out.

~ ~ ~

The Armstrongs checked into the Green Mountain Nudist Resort late in the afternoon of the day they got the assignment. They set up their tent in a site near the camp's front gate in order to keep an eye on all traffic entering and leaving. The next morning, they were at their surveillance post bright and early, but despite the fact that they stuck with it all day, no one resembling either of the suspected perps showed up. They checked with the Albany office and were told to stay one more day and then come home. After forty-eight fruitless hours, special agents Tina and Larry Armstrong folded their tent and went home, with only intimate sunburns to show for their efforts.

~ ~ ~

R. C. McNutt sang a little tune as he drove through the night toward his 2:00 a.m. rendezvous with Baz Rathbone. He had made good time from Scranton and at the moment was passing through the rolling countryside between the

New York towns of East Chatham and New Lebanon. The Massachusetts state line was about five miles to the east of his position. An hour or so earlier, R. C. had stopped on the shoulder of the Taconic State Parkway long enough to take Clyde out of his body bag and prop him up in the passenger's seat of the Smart car. The decaying ape's odor had taken a sharp turn for the worse in the last few hours and R. C. had decided to try airing him out a bit. All of the car's windows were wide open as the two travelers cruised along.

"Born to be wiiild!" sang R.C., wishing he were back in North Carolina driving across the Piedmont instead of hauling a dead ape through New England. He reached into the glove box and pulled out another marijuana joint from his dwindling supply. The last one had almost killed him, but now that he'd gotten rid of the witch-granny's corpse, he was ready to try again. He lit the doobie and took a deep drag. The buzz came on in just a few seconds. "Oh, it's wicked, evil, mean….," sang R. C. in his very best John Kay voice.

He had just turned onto New York Route 22 north, and was half way through his second joint, when he saw the flashing lights in his rear view mirror. "Well, shit!" thought R.C. "Just what I need, a dumb ass country cop. And me with a dead ape riding shotgun. No good can come of this."

Deciding to play it safe – "Maybe I've only got a faulty taillight," he thought – R. C. pulled off into the breakdown lane and stopped. He flicked the joint past Clyde's nose and out the passenger's window. The police cruiser pulled in behind him and shone its spotlight into the Smart car's interior. Then a cop who appeared to be just out of high school got out and wandered up to R. C.'s window.

"Good evening, sir," said the cop. "Are you aware that you were exceeding the speed limit by a good ten miles per hour? These roads are pretty tricky driving at night, what with all the curves. It's a good idea to stick to the posted limit."

Up to this point, the cop had stuck to the routine script for a moving violation. But then simultaneously, he smelled the marijuana fumes coming off R. C.'s clothes and he spotted the dead orangutan. The officer's demeanor changed markedly and not for the better.

"Well, sir, enjoying a little rolling toke, were you? And what's the story on your hairy passenger there? That doesn't look like the family dog to me. I think you'd better get out and show me some identification. You and your sidekick warrant a call to the station, I'd say."

But when the policeman stepped back a pace in anticipation of R. C.'s exit from the Smart car, McNutt panicked and gunned the vehicle down the road. Within seconds, the cop was in hot pursuit and for several miles the two vehicles careened one after the other down the winding country road. Then, sensing that he wasn't going to outrun this guy, R. C. decided on extreme evasive action. Just outside of New Lebanon, he spotted a car dealership and swerved off the highway and into the huge lot. Now the chase was constrained by row after row of cars on display and the greater maneuverability of the Smart car paid off. At the end of each row of display vehicles, R. C. made a screeching turn that neatly reversed his direction into the next aisle. The cop's Crown Vic, on the other hand, had to be laboriously maneuvered from one aisle to the next. "I'm losing him!" thought R. C., even though that was not really the case.

Then he saw a way out. At the end of the aisle nearest the low brick wall fronting the car lot, R. C. saw a display ramp raised to its maximum 20-degree angle. As if it had been left by his guardian angel, the ramp was empty and oriented back toward the highway. "I'm having that!" said R. C. to himself as he sped toward the ramp.

Now, R. C. McNutt had grown up as a big fan of Evel Knievel and he had watched and rewatched every single episode of "The Dukes of Hazzard." For these reasons – plus the marijuana high that he was still enjoying – he thought he knew just about everything there was to know about jumping a car off a ramp and over a fence. He put the Smart car's pedal to the metal.

Just as R. C. had hoped, the zippy little machine shot up the ramp, went airborne, and sailed over the brick wall. It hit the ground on the far side with a thump that caused the passenger's side door to pop open and Clyde to fly out into the night. (The ape had neglected to fasten his seat belt.) R. C. just about bit off the end of his tongue, but he managed to keep control of the car and in a few seconds, he was back on the highway and speeding away.

In contrast to R. C.'s good luck with the ramp, the pursuing officer had a much less pleasant experience. He unwisely decided to try to replicate the Smart car's jump, but because of a difference in speed or vehicle weight, or both, he only managed to jump *onto* the brick wall, not over it. The patrol car sat there, high and dry, as its driver watched the Smart car's taillights recede into the distance. "I am so screwed!" thought the cop. "The Captain's not gonna be happy about this."

And, in fact, the Captain was distinctly *unhappy* when he learned that one of his rookie officers had run a patrol car up onto a brick wall. Nor did it help the unlucky officer's case that the crash scene yielded a dead orangutan that was wanted as evidence by the FBI, as well as by police in both North Carolina and Virginia. The rookie cop's last official act before handing in his resignation the next day was to load the dead ape into the Animal Control Officer's van and, following instructions from the FBI, drive it to the town morgue and put it in cold storage.

CHAPTER NINETEEN

When R. C. McNutt failed to show up at the agreed upon 2:00 a.m. rendezvous in Williamstown, Baz Rathbone had a sinking feeling that the ape skull caper had gone off the rails. Nonetheless, he drove around the sleeping town several times, cruising through the empty Salvation Army parking lot on each pass. Finally, at two-thirty, he found a public phone in an all-night 7-11 and, praying that the iPhone's battery was still functioning, called Annette Fibrowski's cell number. McNutt answered on the second ring.

"McNutt here," said R. C. "Is that you…"

"No names, damn it!" hissed Baz, in a voice loud enough to cause the 7-11 clerk to peer at him around the cigarette display.

"Oh yeah, sorry Baz," said R. C. "Aw shit! I did it again. Sorry."

"You're pathetic, do you know that?" said Baz.

"Well, now that's not a nice thing to say after all we've…," began McNutt, only to be cut off in mid-sentence.

"Shut up, doofus," snapped Baz. "Just tell me where you are and why you missed the drop off."

"Well, uh, it's like this," said R. C., "I didn't swing by and drop off the ape because I no longer have an ape to drop off."

"*What!*" shouted Baz, prompting another quizzical look from the store clerk. "Where – is – the – orang?" he asked with deadly menace.

"OK, here's what happened," said R. C. "Just east of Albany, I got pulled over for speeding and while the cop was deciding whether or not to write me up, he spotted the dead ape and wanted to take me downtown for a chat."

"How the hell could he have spotted the ape?" said Baz. "The ape was in a body bag behind the driver's seat, the last time I heard."

"Well, uh, he was really stinking and so I took him out of

131

the bag and sat him up in the passenger's seat," said R. C., knowing he was about to get the reaming out of a lifetime. "I just wanted to sort of air him out a little, you know?"

"You colossal, stupendous, gaping, flaming ASSHOLE!" choked Baz. "If I ever get my hands on you, I'm going to wring your neck! Jeez! You stupid twit! Oh well, crap, go on with your story, and please don't tell me that you're sitting in an interrogation room right now and that this whole conversation is being taped."

"Aw, no way, man, nothing to worry about there. I got away from that cop. Made him look silly, as a matter of fact. When he stepped away from my car to let me out, I gunned the engine and took off. He chased me for a while, but I pulled into a car dealership and out-maneuvered his big ass Crown Vic up, down, and around the rows of cars. These Smart cars can turn on a dime, I can tell you that."

"So how'd you finally escape?" asked Baz.

"It was beautiful, man," said R. C., "just like in the movies. As I shot down the last aisle at the car lot with the cop hot on my butt, I spotted a display ramp all set up, but empty. I floored the Smart car, hit the ramp going about eighty, and cleared the brick wall that fronted the dealership. The cop made the mistake of hesitating before taking the ramp himself and ended up sitting high and dry on top of the wall. I'm guessing he totaled his cruiser."

"And the ape carcass?" asked Baz. "What happened to the ape carcass in all of this?"

"Well, of course, I never thought I'd have to take spectacular evasive action while the ape was riding shotgun and so I didn't fasten his seatbelt. When I finally hit the ground after sailing over the wall, the ape's door popped open and he fell out. I didn't think it was too smart to stop and go back for him. That cop had a gun and he was some kinda pissed off the last time I saw him."

"So you lost the ape and now I guess you're high-tailing it back south before the New York cops grab your sorry, worthless ass. That right?" signed Baz.

"Actually," said R. C., "I haven't started south just yet. I was hoping we could meet somewhere and you could pay me a portion of my salary. I know you won't want to give me the whole thing, but..."

"*Nothing! Nada! Zip! Zero!*" hissed Baz. "That's how much money you've got coming, you unbelievable little shitbird! You took a simple heist and screwed it up beyond recognition. By my count, you are now guilty of auto theft, kidnapping, body snatching, stealing personal property, speeding, and resisting arrest. If they ever catch you, asshole, they're going to put you away for a long time. And I'll tell you this, if they do catch you and you try to implicate me, I'm going to swear on my mother's grave that I don't know you. I'm not doing time because of your stupidity."

"Careful, now, partner," said R. C. "I can tell them a lot about you if they catch me. We're both better off if we stick together."

"Oh yeah?" said Baz. "You know one of my many aliases, not my real name; you have no idea what I look like; you have no idea where I live or what kind of car I'm driving. My phone numbers and email addresses have all just been changed, and when I get off this phone, I'm flying off for an extended international vacation. How does that make you feel, dumb butt? All alone? Good bye."

R. C. just had time to say "But" when he heard the line go dead. "Well, shit," he thought to himself. "No pay, miles from home, middle of the night. But I suppose things could be worse. They haven't put the cuffs on me yet. And besides, when the going gets tough, the tough smoke dope. I do believe I'll have another joint." He dug around in the glove box, found what he was searching for, and lit up. Then R. C. McNutt swung the Smart car around and headed back to Cousin Raleigh's house via the backest of back roads.

~ ~ ~

It was day six of their big adventure and the three Mainers were just north of Boston on I-95 when Lazlo got a cell phone call from Steve Nevets. The New Lebanon, New York, police, Nevets told him, had recovered the ape carcass. If Lazlo and company didn't mind making a longish detour west via the Mass Pike, they could pick up the animal at their convenience. The New Lebanon people had been instructed to put the ape in cold storage, said the FBI agent.

"Well, this will make four out of five," said Lazlo as he swung onto I-495 at Amesbury and headed southwest.

"How's that?" asked A-Fib from the rear seat.

"One – and most important – we got you back," said Lazlo. "Two, we got the van back. Three, we got Big Mac the crocodile back. And four, we're about to get Clyde back. The only thing – I mean, person – still missing is Mrs. Sagler. Which reminds me that I'm going to get fired when we get home."

"You mean four out of six," corrected Uli. "Don't forget about all those bombers we were carrying in the glove box. I could really go for a smoke about now." His companions all nodded their heads in agreement.

"OK, this detour is going to mean we'll be sleeping on the road one more night," said A-Fib, who had been studying the map. "My best estimate is nine hours of driving time from New Lebanon to Moose Wallow. What do you say we go up to Williamstown, Mass, for the night after we collect Clyde? It's a funky little college town with some good pubs. We used to play William's College in women's field hockey, so I know the town pretty well."

"Sounds good to me," said Uli.

"Me too," said Lazlo. Then turning and looking back at A-Fib, he asked, "How are you feeling, honey? Any lasting effects of being bound, gagged, and hauled around? I really do apologize for all of that, by the way."

"Laz, will you please stop apologizing for the kidnapping?" said Annette. "No way in the world do I blame you for anything – except maybe for being the world's worst snorer. I'm just fine, although I'll probably never forget the taste of that gag, and as you said, when we pick up Clyde, we'll be four for five. I just hope the thieves didn't pitch Mrs. Sagler off a bridge or something awful like that. The poor little woman deserved a decent burial."

"And I hope poor old Clyde hasn't deteriorated so much that I can't do a nice stuffing job," said Uli. "If his hair has started coming out in handfuls, it's going to be tough."

"Ugh," said A-Fib. "I don't know whose job is weirder,

Uli, yours or Lazlo's. Between the two of you, you've got some seriously macabre stuff going on, you know that? My mother always hoped I'd hang out with men who wore suits. She'd look at you two and throw up her hands."

"Suits? *Suits?*" said Uli. "Come on, girl, you know you prefer manly men like Laz and me over dudes wearing suits and smelling of cologne." The "manly men" comment made them all laugh.

"Yeah, OK," said A-Fib. "Forget about the suits. You'll both be my heroes forever if you'll buy me a beer at supper tonight."

"You're on!" said Lazlo and Uli in unison.

~ ~ ~

It wasn't until the day after his computer meltdown that Tom Mot remembered that during the tapped phone conversation he'd heard a new name for the man waiting to receive the ape carcass. He already knew the name Baz Rathbone, of course, as well as Rathbone's email initials, SGM. But when answering the phone on the previous day, the Rathbone/SGM person had identified himself as "Zuber." "Zuber here," he'd said when he picked up the instrument. Zuber: it was a strange name if Mot had ever heard one and in the criminal investigation game, strangeness often paid dividends since it stuck in people's (witnesses, victims) minds. He made a mental note to do some research on the name Zuber using the new laptop he was renting at the Bureau's expense. He would eventually be issued a replacement machine for the one he'd drowned, of course, but processing the paperwork would take months.

In the meantime, it sure looked like Rathbone/SGM/Zuber had gone to ground. That very morning, Mot had tried sending an email to the only address he had for SGM and it had been bounced back. Furthermore, when he'd checked on Norman McLaughlin's (i.e., McHead-Case's) computer for emails to/from SGM, he had found none. Mot strongly suspected that the failure of the ape heist was connected to SGM's disappearance. Damned frustrating, that's what it was. If the guy panicked and skipped the country, they might never catch up with him and months of hard work would have been wasted. Oh well, with no other leads at this point (Mot didn't count R. C. McNutt, who pretty clearly didn't know Rathbone's whereabouts), he'd invest some time researching Zubers.

~ ~ ~

And what, after all this time, of Josie May Sagler? Well, although there was no way she could know it, Mrs. Sagler was in New England and closing the distance to Maine, the beloved state of her birth. And she would have made it too, well within UPS's estimated three-day shipping time from Staunton to Moose Wallow, had not the truck that contained her body taken a right turn off of I-95 at Providence, Rhode Island, and made a beeline for Cape Cod.

The truck was just doing what it was supposed to do; the driver had not made an error. No, the error that now had Josie May headed to Martha's Vineyard was a labeling mistake that had occurred in a distribution center near Washington, D. C. Two items scheduled for delivery to customers named Wetzo – one a coffee maker and the other Josie May – had crossed paths at that center. In the middle-of-the-night frenzy of unloading, checking, weighing, and rerouting, the Staunton UPS label, as well as most of the handmade address label that R. C. McNutt had affixed to Mrs. Sagler's box, had been torn off. The sole remnant read simply, "Wetzo....MA." (Unfortunately, R. C. had sowed the initial seeds of confusion back in Virginia when he wrote out Maine's abbreviation as MA, not the correct form, ME.) The over-worked and under-interested shipping agent had assumed that both the coffee maker and the larger package were going to the same Wetzo ("How many Wetzos can there be?" he had thought) and so he filled out a new address label for the big box using information from the small one. The next day, Artie Wetzo, resident of Menemsha village on the Vineyard's western end and uncle of Lazlo Wetzo, found himself signing for a new Krups coffee maker and (although he didn't know it) for a human body.

CHAPTER TWENTY

Bart Zuber (Baz Rathbone), although usually a cool customer, was starting to get panicky. Even long rides on his motorcycle through the spring scenery of Mt. Mansfield State Forest failed to calm his soul. Somehow the Akwesasne Mohawks had located him in Upper Gooseberry and their threats about unpaid gambling debts were starting to get downright nasty. Additionally, he owed money on his mortgage, his backhoe, his utility bills, and the grocery and bar tabs he was running at various establishments around town. Financially speaking, he was in deep shit and now that the ape heist had fallen through, he could see no way out.

Damn that McNutt! What a complete screw-up he'd made of the ape job! That carcass could have netted thousands of dollars, Baz was certain of that. Perhaps it could have come close to solving his financial woes. But good old Asshole McNutt had let the orangutan slip through his fingers, or more correctly, he'd let it fly out the car door. Baz swore that if he got out of this without jail time, he'd never trust a redneck again.

But the odds of avoiding jail time seemed to be getting smaller and smaller. Since he and McNutt had technically been criminal collaborators, Baz knew he could be implicated to some extent in auto and personal property theft, kidnapping, and body snatching. Worse yet, he had shot himself in the foot long ago by making contact with that Captain Kidd person, who he'd bet a-dollar-to-a-doughnut was the cop who tapped his phone. It seemed like a good time to cut bait, disappear entirely for a while, and resurface when the heat was off.

OK, so where to start? Baz racked his brain (which didn't take all that long). He had a small inventory of body parts on hand: three prepared human skulls, a bobcat skull, a wolf skull (in reality, a large German Shepard), and the fossilized tooth of a mastodon. The last, although a clear departure from his usual sale items, was in beautiful condition and thus worth thousands of dollars to the right collector. Baz made the decision to take a chance and get back online long enough to advertise a going-out-of-business sale. It was a risky thing to do, but desperate times call for desperate measures.

He sat down at his computer and registered with Google for yet another Gmail account under yet another alias. He created a new username and password, and then sent an email to a half dozen reliable customers.

> FROM: Director,
> justtryingtogetahead.com
> TO: McHead-Case@gmail.com
> BCC: Skullboy@yahoo.com,
> Occipital@gmail.com,
> Sagittalcrestme@gmail.com
> SUBJECT: Final sales
>
> Dear friends:
> I have decided to leave the skull business and pursue other interests. At present, I have three human skulls (all fully prepared and perfect), a beautiful bobcat skull, a wolf skull (fangs intact), and a fossilized mastodon tooth (reputed to have been found alongside a Clovis point). If you are interested in any of these items, please contact me within 48 hours by return email for prices. I look forward to hearing from you.
> Sincerely,
> SGM

The die was cast. Baz began researching countries lacking extradition agreements with the United States. Cuba immediately jumped to the top of the list. "Hell," thought Baz, "I even speak a little Spanish."

~ ~ ~

Artie Wetzo had seen death in his time. He'd sent any number of small dogs to the Great Beyond by feeding them to his friend Mike Uxum's piranha fish and he'd even watched in horror as those same fish consumed Mike's uncle and Artie's pal, Leroi Uxum (on Leroi's birthday, no less). Yes, Artie had watched, even helped, the Grim Reaper's work without flinching, but that didn't keep him from flinching when he unwrapped Mrs. Josie May Sagler.

Neither Artie nor his wife, Wanda, could remember ordering anything from Staunton, Virginia, which was where the large box in front of them had been mailed. Still, one does so much online shopping these days, they figured they'd just lost track of some largish purchase. Artie went to his shop and got a utility knife, and together they cut into the box.

Their first glimpse of the contents was a mass of curly black hair encased in bubble wrap and clear packing tape. That was enough for Wanda, who squealed "Dead monkey!" and jumped about six feet backwards.

"What are you talking about, Wanda?" said Artie, who also had the heebie-jeebies, but was damned if he'd let it show. "That's no monkey. Monkey hair is straighter than that. There are some pigs with curly hair, but I'm guessing this is not a pig. I'd better keeping cutting."

Three more whacks with the utility knife and the bubble wrap parted to reveal Josie May's head and shoulders. Now it was Artie's turn to jump back and he exceeded his wife's record by a good two feet.

"Holy shit, Wanda! Somebody has sent us a *corpse!* That lady is not breathing and hasn't been for a while. And – *Jeez Louise!* – whoever stuck her in that box made sure you'd look straight down her pink nightie when you opened her up! What kind of sick joke is this?"

"I'm not staying in the same house with a special delivery dead woman, Artie Wetzo," said Wanda. "You get that thing – that person – out of here and then call the police."

Artie knew good advice when he heard it. He closed up Josie May's box and dragged it out to the garage. Then he came back inside and made two phone calls: the first to Lieutenant Jim Hennessy down at the Menemsha police station, and the second to his friend Moe Thibault, an ordained minister in the Church of Seismology. The woman might be dead, reasoned Artie, but it was still possible she'd be comforted by the presence of a minister.

Jim Hennessy was just a few blocks down Menemsha's Main Street from the Wetzos' home and so he was the first to arrive. Using gloved hands, he examined the box carefully and also what he could see of Mrs. Sagler.

"I've heard of junk mail, Artie, but this takes the cake," bad-joked the policeman. "Did you handle it too, Wanda? I need to know so I can tell the crime lab people whose fingerprints we can be sure they'll find."

"I touched the top a little, Lieutenant," said Wanda, who looked like she was considering throwing up. "I wish I hadn't now, but we didn't see that poor woman until we got through the first couple of layers of packaging."

"All right," said Hennessy, "I'm going to call the forensic people over at the main station in Chilmark, so just leave everything as it is. I'm also going to call the Virginia State Police to see if they have any missing person cases going on. Better put on a pot of coffee, Wanda. The crime scene investigators are always thirsty and, besides, it'll give you something to do."

As Hennessy was putting in calls for assistance and Wanda was making coffee, Moe Thibault pulled up in front of the Wetzos' house. An octogenarian of surprising physical vigor – but whose mind sometimes slipped a notch, leaving him believing he was Inspector Jacques Clouseau or Rudyard Kipling – Moe gave a yell as he came up the walk. "Hey, Artie! Wanda! It's me, Moe!"

"Hi Moe," said Artie. "We just got a dead person by UPS. Want to see?" Moe indicated that he did and so Artie took him through to the garage and pointed him toward the box. "Lieutenant Hennessy said not to touch anything, Moe," cautioned Artie.

Moe peered into the box and then leaned down and gave the corpse a sniff.

"I do believe you're right, Artie. The Force is no longer with the person in that box. I hope she didn't suffocate on her way here. You probably noted that there are no air holes in the box's sides. That could be significant."

"Jeez, Moe," said Artie admiringly, "you never cease to amaze me. I'd missed that detail completely, but I'll sure point it out to the cops when they come back."

"There you go, Dr. Watson," said Moe.

"Listen, Moe, do you think that poor woman needs the last rites or something like that? Does the Church of Seismology have last rites? As a Senior Richter Minister, you know that stuff better than I do," said Artie.

Moe thought about it for a second and then said, "Well, she *is* all bundled up like those folks in Pompeii, but otherwise there's no evidence that she died in an earthquake or volcanic eruption. And if she's a Methodist or Baptist and I start praying over her in the name of the great god Yolanda, she's going to get awful confused. All in all, I'd say the best thing is to leave her be and assume she got last rites back in – where'd you say she came from? – oh yeah, Virginia."

As the two men stood in the garage discussing the strange case of the mail order corpse, Jim Hennessy returned, accompanied by his forensics team.

"OK, guys," said Jim, "let's go inside and give these boys room to work. They're going to dust the box for fingerprints and since it's undoubtedly been handled many times between here and Staunton, it's going to take a while. Oh, and by the way, I'm pretty sure I know who she is and where she was going. The Virginia State Police told me that the body of Mrs. Josie May Sagler was stolen a couple of days ago down in North Carolina. She was taken from a van owned by – you're gonna love this, Artie – one Lazlo Wetzo, who was transporting Mrs. Sagler's body back to Maine for burial. You never told me you had a relative in the funeral business, Artie."

"Oh, yeah, Lazlo," said Artie. "He's my brother's kid. I think he's only been up in Maine for six months or so. My brother and sister-in-law were glad when he got a job and finally left home. You don't think Lazlo's done anything illegal, do you, Lieutenant?"

"Nah," said the policeman. "His van was swiped and all of its contents taken. The Virginia State Police are in contact with both North Carolina and the FBI to see if they can't arrange for Lazlo to come retrieve Mrs. Sagler and finish the delivery to Maine. They think he is somewhere in upstate New York right now picking up a dead orangutan."

"Holy moly!" said Artie. "Dead people, dead apes, and my nephew Lazlo – are you as confused as I am, Moe?"

"I am, indeed, Artie, and I feel the need for a powerful stimulant. Do you have Scotch whisky in the house, my man? You do? Excellent. Lead me to it and then I'll offer a prayer to Yolanda for Mrs. What's-Her-Name's life."

Early the next afternoon, Lazlo, Uli, A-Fib, and their van full of weird wonders pulled off the ferry that ran between Wood's Hole and Vineyard Haven. They drove to Menemsha, picked up Mrs. Sagler (putting her in a more appropriate transport container than the U-Haul box), had a late lunch with Artie and Wanda, and then resumed their zigzag journey back to Moose Wallow. Once again, Lazlo's van was filled to capacity with three live people, one human corpse, one ape carcass, and a stuffed crocodile in need of cosmetic taxidermy. The three live travelers all vowed that if they ever got back to Maine, it would be a long time before they ventured out again.

CHAPTER TWENTY ONE

Baz Rathbone was wrapping it up. He had heard back from Norman McLaughlin almost immediately and was delighted to learn that McHead-Case wanted to buy everything Baz had on offer. Norman had recently been promoted to Shift Supervisor at his surgical job and he was feeling flush. The three new human heads, the bobcat skull, and the "wolf" skull would fill the remaining display space in Norman's Bone Room 3. He planned to show off the mastodon tooth in a purpose-built lighted display case in his living room. The purchase was going to cost him a bundle, but he was OK with that.

For his part, Baz Rathbone was more than OK with the prospect of dumping his remaining inventory in one fell swoop and doing business with a buyer who lived relatively close by. Maybe he'd break with tradition and deliver the goods in person, thought Baz. The whole shipment would be light and compact enough to load onto the back of his Harley. The ride from Upper Gooseberry, Vermont, due east to Bangor, Maine, looked interesting. There were supposed to be some beautiful gorges in the Nash Stream Forest area and this would be a chance to see them. He exchanged a series of emails with McHead-Case arranging the details of the delivery – date and time, place, and method of payment. The euphoria of getting out of the bone business, selling his property in Upper Gooseberry, and moving to a tropical island with no U. S. extradition agreement was having the effect of making Baz less cautious than normal. He would come to regret it, but at the moment he couldn't see how anything could go wrong. Ten days from now, he'd be sitting in a Havana bar drinking a Cuba Libre.

~ ~ ~

Unbeknownst to Baz, Tom Mot and Steve Nevets knew every detail of his going-out-of-business sale and many other things, as well. Thanks to Mot's skill as a hacker, they had used Norman McLaughlin's link to the person they originally knew only as SGM to tap directly into the Baz's computer. Now, in addition to his email persona, they knew that he used at least two business aliases, Baz Rathbone and somebody Zuber. They knew what he liked to read, what movies he liked to watch ("tsk, tsk"), that he owned a late model Chevy truck and a Harley-Davidson motorcycle, and that he changed his email username and password *very* frequently. They knew that Rathbone/Zuber lived in Upper Gooseberry, Vermont, and that his rendezvous with Norman McLaughlin was set for three in the afternoon on May 15th at an old family campground on Great Pond near Waterville, Maine. (As Baz knew from boyhood visits, in mid-May all of the Belgrade Lake camps have yet to be opened for the summer and the road back to the lakeside lodge of Camp Bellweather was long and secluded. He and McLaughlin were scheduled to meet in the camp's parking area, make their exchange, and then go their separate ways. It was going to be like falling off a log.)

The other important pieces of information that the two FBI agents knew about Rathbone/Zuber was that he had recently listed his property with a real estate agent and that he had advertised a backhoe for sale on eBay. Everything pointed toward Rathbone/Zuber getting ready to make a run for it. But how best to bust him? Nevets and Mot differed on the best plan of action.

"I say we drive to this Upper Gooseberry place right now and collar the guy," argued Mot. "We've got plenty of evidence that he was part of the robbery and kidnapping down in North Carolina. The email connections to the skull trade should be enough to tie him into that."

"Well, it's true what you say about the North Carolina thing," said Nevets, "but I'd be a lot happier if we could also catch him red-handed selling human body parts. Then we'd absolutely have enough charges to put him away for a long time. I think we should wait until he meets up with McLaughlin at this camp near Waterville. We can put a microphone on the buyer and listen to the whole thing."

"All right, Steve, I can live with that," said Mot. "I'm just super ready to wrap up this case and go home. If I have to stay in one more motel named the Dew Drop Inn or Moosehead Manor, I'm gonna go nuts."

"I hear you, partner," said Nevets. "OK, you keep monitoring Rathbone's email messages and I'll get in touch with McLaughlin about wearing a wire. It'll be good to have a visual on McLaughlin anyway, so we don't arrest the wrong man."

~ ~ ~

In Upper Gooseberry, things were starting to move at warp speed for Baz. Within three days of listing his cabin and land on Roaring Goose Creek, he had an offer and a deposit. A landscape painter from New York City and her photographer husband thought the property would be perfect as the mountain retreat they'd always wanted. Both were charmed by the seclusion of the property and the views along the creek. While the wife eyed the interior of the cabin for studio space, her shutterbug husband laid claim to the secondhand shed that Baz had installed atop a patch of disturbed ground that had been newly leveled. With the addition of electric and water connections, the shed would do quite well as a rustic darkroom.

The backhoe had sold almost immediately, as well. A landscaper over the mountain had snapped it up the day after the shed installation was finished. And finally, the office furnishings of Zuber's Affordable Cremations in Upper Gooseberry had either been sold at a profit or returned to the original vendors, and Baz had removed the sign over the storefront's door.

Baz's actual departure from the cabin on Roaring Goose Creek had to be delayed for a few days so he could finish preparing the last shipment of skulls. The five skulls he would be selling to Norman McLaughlin – three human specimens, one "wolf," and one bobcat – had been defleshed by placing them in large rubber tubs containing dermestid beetles. After all muscles, tendons, and other tissue had been consumed by these tireless flesh-eaters, Baz had washed the skulls carefully and then bleached them in hydrogen peroxide for twenty-four hours. If McLaughlin wanted to do anything more before putting them on display – put a finishing coat of varnish on them, for example – that was his business. Baz ended his preparations with bleaching and drying. Then he packed each specimen in its own small box for transport and when he was done, he taped the six boxes together (five skulls plus one mastodon tooth) to produce a parcel sufficiently small to be carried comfortably behind him on the motorcycle.

~ ~ ~

Early on the morning of May 15th, three separate parties began their journeys toward Great Pond and Camp Bellweather: Steve Nevets and Tom Mot, driving from their current location in lower New Hampshire; Norman McLaughlin, driving from his home near Bangor, Maine; and Baz Rathbone, riding his Harley from far northern Vermont. Baz had calculated that the trip would take him just over five hours to complete, but because he wanted to enjoy a leisurely run on his Sportster through the Nash Stream Forest gorges, he had started just after sunrise.

Despite the fact that he was traveling on secondary roads, Baz made good time, and by ten-thirty he was crossing US-3 and approaching the Nash Stream Area. It was a gorgeous day and he was enjoying the ride tremendously. His motorcycle was performing perfectly, there was little traffic on the back roads, and so far he'd only had one massive bug splatter itself across his visor. Life was good.

Unhappily for Baz, his life was not only good at that moment, but also drawing to a close. As he entered the first of the Nash Stream gorges, he rounded a sharp turn and came face to face with a white truck filled with appliances on their way to new owners. The truck's driver was cruising down the middle of the road as he fiddled with his cell phone, obviously annoyed by the fact that he'd just driven into a "dead zone." He didn't see the motorcycle until it was swerving crazily trying to avoid a head-on collision. Making a quick swerve of his own, the truck driver missed the bike and continued around the next turn, unaware that he had just caused a fatal accident.

Baz Rathbone was a good rider; there was no question

about that. He had logged in thousands of hours on his Harley and he'd had his share of near misses. And he would have successfully avoided a crash this time had it not been for his wandering eye and the possum that was crossing the road just around the next bend. "A possum?" thought Baz as he spotted the animal. "What the hell's a possum doing in the road?" Or were there *two* possums? He was moving so fast that his good eye and bad eye couldn't agree either on the number of possums in his path or on its (their) exact position(s). Making a second drastic swerve just as he was regaining control of the bike proved impossible. Baz hit the possum squarely in the short ribs and the impact caused the motorcycle to careen toward the guardrail. His last thought as he and his cargo of skulls flew off of the crumpled motorcycle, over the railing, and into the gorge was, "Well, fuck! Killed by a possum! What kind of stupid way to die is that?"

It is not necessary to go into the results of Baz's crash in gory detail. Suffice it to say that it was fatal and that despite the fact that poetic justice would have been served had his head been detached from his body, it was not. A passing car spotted the remains of the motorcycle and called 911. After some effort by the New Hampshire State Police and local EMTs, Baz and his cargo were recovered from the bottom of the gorge. Although CPR was attempted, he was ruled dead at the scene.

~ ~ ~

By 5:00 p.m., agents Nevets and Mot, along with Norman McLaughlin – who was wearing a hidden microphone, into which he kept saying, "Testing, testing" – had been waiting at Camp Bellweather for several hours. When Rathbone was two full hours late for the meet-up, Nevets put in calls to the Vermont, New Hampshire, and Maine state police to see if they knew anything about the skull dealer's whereabouts. The call to New Hampshire hit pay dirt, and Nevets was told that a man on a motorcycle carrying a collection of human and animal skulls had been killed in a traffic accident in the western part of the state. He'd been wearing a leather jacket bearing the logo "Born to

Cremate" when the accident occurred.

"Do you think this is the guy you've been searching for?" asked Sergeant Gary Peterson, who had been Nevets and Mot's New Hampshire State Police contact person for months.

"Most likely," said Nevets. "We've never laid eyes on the guy, but the fact that he was carrying a load a skulls and wearing a "Born to Cremate" jacket tells me he was our man. We're over in Maine with the buyer. The contract was for five skulls, three of them human, and a fossilized mastodon tooth, which matches your inventory at the crash scene. I think you guys just scraped up our perp."

"Yeah, probably," said Peterson. "Oh well, the body and cargo will be waiting for you at the Troop F barracks in Twin Mountain. I'll tell them to be expecting you."

"Thanks, Gary," said Nevets. "Tell them to save us a couple of doughnuts."

While Nevets was on the phone to the NHSP, Mot was arranging for the two of them to make a visit to see Norman McLaughlin's skull collection. Although it seemed unlikely (and subsequently proved to be the case) that the single human skull McLaughlin had bought from Baz Rathbone could be traced back to a specific instance of corpse abuse and fraud, still the FBI needed to check it out. Norman readily agreed to the visit. Heck, nothing this exciting had ever happened to him before. As long as he wasn't being charged with a crime, he was perfectly happy to hang out with his new FBI friends.

CHAPTER TWENTY TWO

It took almost no time for the FBI to figure out from his facial features and fingerprints that the dealer in human (and other) skulls had been none other than Percy Sanders – aka Baz Rathbone, Bart Zuber, and SGM – a small time crook with a rap sheet that included food stamp trafficking, beano game violations, cheating and swindling for less than $1000, and impersonating a state lottery official. He had expanded into felonious crimes with corpse abuse and fraud.

The first thing agents Nevets and Mot did after learning Sanders' identity was to visit his former property in Upper Gooseberry. They found nothing suspicious in the house, but in the newly compacted and leveled ground under the shed, they found the headless bodies of half a dozen people. Then, using multiple photographs of Sanders – one from his corpse and several others from mug shots – they expanded their search for his earlier bases of operation. In Rankin, New York, they found what they were looking for. Several people there recognized Baz Rathbone as the man in the photos. Yes, they said, he had lived and worked in Rankin until just a few months ago. He had run a cut-rate cremation service called PWADS, they recalled, and had lived on a farm up in Owl Hollow.

Upon investigation, the Owl Hollow farm, like the property on Roaring Goose Creek, was found to have a sizable area of ground that looked to have been dug up fairly recently. Excavations revealed several dozen headless bodies, some of which appeared to have been there for years. In response to inquiries around Rankin, several former customers of PWADS came forward, including one – Mrs. Edna Blyth – who stated that her dead husband had had identifiable features of the lower body: a club foot on the right side and also missing fingers on his left hand from a hunting accident. After forensic experts had sorted out the Owl Hollow bodies and the remains described above were available to be shown to Mrs. Blyth, she was able to identify them as belonging to her late husband, Mortimer. Asked to bring in her husband's cremains for analysis, Mrs. Blyth produced a small urn full of wood ashes.

Nevets and Mot were satisfied that they had solved the case of the skull trafficking mortician, though, of course, due to Sanders/Rathbone/Zuber/SGM's untimely death, they could never press charges. Leaving it to the forensic people to sort out the rest of the skeletons, match them as best they could with other defrauded PWADS customers, and reunite the living with what was left of their dead, Nevets and Mot returned to the Boston field office feeling like they had done a good day's work. Their only regret was that they'd been unable to reunite the original complainant, Mrs. Alice Brady – who was also found to possess only a jar of wood ashes – with the remains of her late husband, Herman. Herman had had no interesting features from the neck down, said Alice ("Ouch!" thought Tom Mot), and besides, because she was doing drugs at the time, she still couldn't remember where they were living when he died. Agents Nevets and Mot decided not to lose any sleep over that particular untied loose end.

And as Steve Nevets related to Lazlo Wetzo in a wrap-up phone call to Styx's Riverside Mortuary, the loose end involving R. C. McNutt was tied up very soon after the heist and kidnapping in North Carolina. After jumping his Smart car over the brick wall and eluding the New Lebanon, New York, police, McNutt drove south as fast as he could in an attempt to return the car to his cousin before dropping out of sight. Unfortunately, there aren't that many blue Smart cars on the road and after an APB was issued on R. C., he was quickly scooped up in Pennsylvania. In an attempt to plea-bargain his crimes down to lesser charges, R. C. spilled his guts about the robbery and kidnapping, Baz Rathbone's identity and involvement, his pal Foley Wilson's part in the crimes, and even his cousin Raleigh McNutt's assistance regarding vehicles. Apparently under the mistaken assumption that riddling Big Mac with bullets was high on the list of the charges against him, R. C. told the Easton,

Pennsylvania, cops that, "Foley was the one who shot up the gator. I wasn't carrying a gun. I don't like guns or the NRA. And I'd never, ever shoot an animal. I love animals, all of them! Never even eat meat." His words were wasted, however, both then and at his subsequent trial. After all the legal wrangling was over, both R. C. McNutt and Foley Wilson ended up serving long prison sentences for their parts in the theft of Lazlo's van, robbery of its contents, kidnapping of Annette Fibrowski, and, in R.C.'s case, mistreatment of Mrs. Josie May Sagler's embalmed body. Raleigh McNutt went to jail too, both as a minor accomplice in the Lazlo Wetzo case and because of the evidence of identity theft found in the Smart car when R. C. was arrested. No UPS employees were charged with a crime, although several were severely reprimanded by the company for their part in the shipment of a human corpse.

"We appreciate your help in solving this case, Lazlo," said Nevets as their phone conversation neared its end. "You, Ms. Fibrowski, and Mr. Helmsman all made significant contributions to its successful conclusion. I'm sorry it got so scary for you guys at times, particularly Ms. Fibrowski. Is she OK?"

"A-Fib? Yeah, she's good," said Lazlo. "It takes more than a little kidnapping to get her down. She's a tough lady."

"Well, I'm glad to hear it," said Nevets. "Please give her and Mr. Helmsman our best regards, and if you're ever in the Boston area, give me a call and I'll show you around our field office. Just don't walk in smelling like pot, OK?"

"Yeah, right," said Lazlo with a weak laugh. "Thanks, Agent Nevets."

"Who was that?" asked the very same A-Fib when Lazlo put down the phone.

"Oh, that was the FBI giving me the details of the various trials," said Lazlo. "R. C. McNutt, Raleigh McNutt, and Foley Wilson are all off to jail for the foreseeable future. Steve Nevets asked me to thank you for your help with the case. He also asked if you're OK. I said 'yes,' which is right, isn't it?"

"Perfectly correct," said A-Fib "I've even toothbrushed my tongue enough times so I can't taste that gag anymore."

"I'm glad you're OK, honey," said Lazlo, giving her a hug, "really glad. I was terrified there for a while that I'd lost you."

"And was that so very terrifying?" asked A-Fib mischievously.

"It sure was," said Lazlo. Then summoning his nerve, he broached the subject that had been on his mind for a while. "Listen, A-Fib, have you ever considered being a mortician's wife?"

"Lazlo Yastrzemski Wetzo, are you asking me to marry you?" said A-Fib, drawing back a little to look him squarely in the eyes.

"Yes. Yes, I am," said Lazlo. "I know I'm not much of a catch, but I love you dearly and will try to be a good husband. What about it?"

"Well," said A-Fib, deliberately drawing out her answer to keep Lazlo in suspense, "I *will* marry you, but not just yet."

"What does that mean?" asked the bewildered Lazlo.

"It means that I intend to go down to the U. Maine campus in Augusta and get my Master's degree in social work. That will take a year or so and then I'll be happy to marry you, with just one condition."

"What does that mean?" asked Lazlo for the second time.

"It means you have to go get examined by a good ear, nose, and throat doctor, sweetie. I think you've got a nose full of polyps and if we can get rid of them, your snoring will stop. It's bad, Lazlo. We've got to do something about it."

"Of course I'll do that, honey!" said Lazlo. "So are we officially engaged?"

"Yup, officially engaged," said A-Fib with a smile that just about blinded Lazlo. "You may kiss your fiancé."

Lazlo was in the middle of doing that very thing when Ron Styx walked in on them. Sensing that this was more celebration than a casual smooch, he asked, "What's up?"

"We just got engaged!" said A-Fib and Lazlo simultaneously, before dissolving into laughter.

"Well, congratulations!" said Ron Styx. "That's great! I hope you'll be very happy. When's the wedding?"

"Not for a year or so," said A-Fib. "I want to go down to

Augusta and get a MSW degree before we tie the knot."

"Are you going to go with her, Laz?" asked Ron.

"Gee, I hadn't thought about it," sputtered Lazlo. "Everything's moving so fast that we haven't thought it through."

"The reason I ask," said Ron, "is because the Augusta office of Styx's Mortuary could use a branch manager and head mortician. Any chance you'd be interested in that position, Lazlo?"

"Wow! Would I!" whooped Lazlo, as A-Fib danced around the office clapping her hands. "That would solve everything! Thanks, Ron! Wow!" And then it was Ron Styx's turn to get a big kiss from Annette.

"I feel so, so overwhelmed," said Lazlo, shaking his head and clearly on the verge of tears. A-Fib moved into action.

"Sit down right here and breathe deeply, Laz," she said, guiding him to a chair. "No cataplexy right now, please. Man oh man, are we ever going to have to work with you before the wedding. I don't want you keeling over when I say, 'I do.'"

"Right, right," said Lazlo, inhaling with all his might.

"But what will you do without Laz here at Riverside, Ron?" asked A-Fib.

"I'll bet Uli Helmsman would be willing to come in occasionally and give me a hand as needed," said Ron. "It might let him get out of the abattoir business as a supplement to his taxidermy. I'll give him a call right now. Why don't you two go out and have a celebratory lunch? I'm sure everything will work out."

And everything *did* work out. A-Fib went off to grad school with Lazlo at her side. Lazlo went off to a new job with more responsibility and more money than he had ever had, and Uli agreed to assist Ron Styx at Riverside whenever he was needed. After all, thought Uli, he'd have some extra time after Big Mac was repaired and returned to South of the Border, and Clyde had been stuffed and touched up (Foley's bullet hole between the eyes needed filling) and returned to the Southlands Zoo. And he sure wouldn't miss killing pigs. Yep, the future looked bright all around. "Time for a toke," said Uli to himself as he reached under the counter for the joint jar.

~ ~ ~

Josie May Sagler was laid to rest in Fort Kent, Maine, in mid-June. Her grave sat atop a bluff overlooking the St. John River and provided a wonderful view of Canada on the far side. Her family had gathered from far and wide for the interment, and included Marvin and Cissy Sagler, who had come up from Hilton Head. It had been a long and strange final journey for Josie May, from the heat and humidity of coastal South Carolina to the cool, dry air of Maine. She hadn't liked that cardboard box part one bit, but no one had listened when she'd complained. Now she could stretch out and enjoy all eternity. Certain that her pink Dior peignoir had been arranged so that just a hint of cleavage showed, she lay back and relaxed.

Acknowledgements

The reactions to my first two works of fiction, *Fish Food* (2013) and *Uncle Moe and the Martha's Vineyard Frackers* (2014), have varied widely, to say the least. Some readers have slapped me on the back and said they laughed until they cried, and one fan even went so far as to suggest that *Fish Food* should be made into a stage play (admittedly, that person identified closely with the character Velma Trailer). Additionally, a gift shop in Asheville has taken the books under its wings and offers them for sale along with those of other Western North Carolina authors. All of these things are highly gratifying.

On the flip side, however, some people who I know have read my work now look at me in a pitying sort of way, as if they can see clear signs of early senility, and a local writer and friend sent me a list of descriptors for my books including "disturbing and demented." (Since that person also said they were "hilarious, unpredictable, and original," I take it to be a tie.) Also of concern, very few members of my family now ask when my next volume is coming out and I'm still waiting to be featured in *The New York Times Sunday Book Review*.

Still, as a P. G. Wodehouse character once said, "I can take some roughs with the smooth" and all in all, I'm still having fun dreaming up weird characters and getting them into trouble or love or both—hence the present volume. Once again, I have been fortunate to have Joy Franklin as my copy editor. The woman is seriously good at her work and a wonderfully pleasant colleague to boot. Thank you, Joy. Thanks also to the hard working staff of Absolutely Amazing eBooks, especially Shirrel Rhoades and Chuck Newman. And finally, throughout the *Mortician* project I've been supported by the love and patience of my wife, Kent M. Loy. Her laughter at my work gives me encouragement and her silence sends me back to the word processor. Thanks, SuKent. Love you madly.

Jim Loy
Hendersonville, NC
September 2015

Thank you for reading.
Please review this book. Reviews help others find Absolutely Amazing eBooks and inspire us to keep providing these marvelous tales.

If you would like to be put on our email list to receive updates on new releases, contests, and promotions, please go to AbsolutelyAmazingEbooks.com and sign up.

About the Author

James D. Loy was born in Knoxville, Tennessee, and educated at the University of Tennessee (BS) and Northwestern University (MA, PhD). He taught physical anthropology at the University of Rhode Island from 1974-2010 and for twenty-five years, he studied and wrote about the social behavior of monkeys. In the mid-1990s, however, unable to think of anything else he wanted to know about monkeys, Jim shifted his research interests to a biography of Charles Darwin's wife (J. D. Loy and Kent M. Loy, 2010, *Emma Darwin: A Victorian Life*, University Press of Florida). In 2010, the Loys moved to Hendersonville, NC, where they are enjoying retirement in the beautiful Appalachian Mountains. When Jim isn't writing or working around the house, he is busy trying to learn Change Ringing on the tower bells of St. James Episcopal Church.

The New Atlantian Library

NewAtlantianLibrary.com
or AbsolutelyAmazingEbooks.com
or AA-eBooks.com

www.ingramcontent.com/pod-product-compliance
Lightning Source LLC
Chambersburg PA
CBHW050408030726
47503CB00006B/2083